*He handed Ver*___ *shoes with a wry smile. "Don't lose one, Cinderella," he teased.*

She snatched them back. "You know, your cousin Candace didn't like you very much."

"Now there's a shock," he said, leading her up the mansion's sweeping front steps.

"She said you're mean, stubborn and ruthless… and will do anything to get your clients off."

"Never a good thing in a lawyer," he said drily.

She met his amused gaze, so strong and confident. Not to mention devoid of shadiness or deceit. With a sinking feeling, she suddenly knew the slain heiress had been completely wrong about him. She shouldn't be surprised. The rivalry between the Rothchild family cousins was legendary in Vegas.

"Touché," Vera acknowledged, thinking just maybe *she'd* been wrong about Conner, too.

Not good. She did *not* want to like this man. Bad enough she was hopelessly attracted to him. What if he turned out to be honorable and principled, too?

He ushered her inside. "Welcome to my home."

Said the spider to the fly.

Dear Reader,

What little girl hasn't dreamed of being Cinderella, swept away by a handsome Prince Charming? But as grown women, we know things like that just don't happen…or do they?

In the glitzy, glamorous world of Las Vegas, anything is possible! Even for a poor girl from the wrong side of the tracks, trapped by circumstances in a life not of her choosing.

Just like Las Vegas, Silhouette novels are all about hope and dreams. Dreams of love and fulfillment, and finding that perfect partner to share your life with. For sixty years, Harlequin and Silhouette Books have brought women like you and me stories of passion and commitment. Stories that touch your heart and make your pulse pound just a little faster.

I am so proud that my books have been a small part of those sixty years of romantic adventures, and am looking forward to writing a lot more stories for you during the next sixty years!

Meanwhile, immerse yourself in the continuing saga of the Las Vegas Rothchilds as they pursue the mystery of the Tears of the Quetzal, the diamond ring that leaves starstruck lovers in its wake, and fulfills the romantic dreams of those who are worthy.

Good reading!

Nina

NINA BRUHNS

Prince Charming for 1 Night

Silhouette®
Romantic
SUSPENSE

Special thanks and acknowledgment to Nina Bruhns for her contribution to the Love in 60 Seconds miniseries

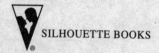

SILHOUETTE BOOKS

ISBN-13: 978-0-373-27638-7

Recycling programs
for this product may
not exist in your area.

PRINCE CHARMING FOR 1 NIGHT

Visit Silhouette Books at www.eHarlequin.com

Printed in U.S.A.

Books by Nina Bruhns

Silhouette Romantic Suspense

Catch Me If You Can #990
Warrior's Bride #1080
Sweet Revenge #1163
Sins of the Father #1209
Sweet Suspicion #1277
Ghost of a Chance #1319
Blue Jeans and a Badge #1361

Hard Case Cowboy #1385
Enemy Husband #1402
Royal Betrayal #1424
The Forbidden Enchantment #1454
Top-Secret Bride #1480
The Rebel Prince #1504
Killer Temptation #1516
Prince Charming for 1 Night #1568

Silhouette Nocturne

Night Mischief #25

NINA BRUHNS

credits her Gypsy great-grandfather for her great love of adventure. She has lived and traveled all over the world, including a six-year stint in Sweden. She has been on scientific expeditions from California to Spain to Egypt and Sudan, and has two graduate degrees in archaeology (with a specialty in Egyptology). She speaks four languages and writes a mean hieroglyphics!

But Nina's first love has always been writing. For her, writing for Silhouette Books is the ultimate adventure. Drawing on her many experiences gives her stories a colorful dimension, and allows her to create settings and characters out of the ordinary. She has won numerous awards for her previous titles, including the prestigious National Readers' Choice Award, three Daphne DuMaurier Awards of Excellence for Overall Best Romantic Suspense of the year, five Dorothy Parker Awards and two Golden Heart Awards, among many others.

A native of Canada, Nina grew up in California and currently resides in Charleston, South Carolina, with her husband and three children. She loves to hear from her readers, and can be reached at P.O. Box 2216, Summerville, SC, 29484-2216 or by e-mail via her Web site at www.NinaBruhns.com, or via the Harlequin Web site at www.eharlequin.com.

To Dorothy McFalls, Judy Watts
and Vicki Sweatman: wonderful friends,
insightful critiquers, amazing writers
and rockin' concert buddies!

Chapter 1

"Hey, Vera, whatcha think?"

Vera Mancuso—or as the patrons of the Diamond Lounge gentlemen's club knew her, Vera LaRue—glanced over at her friend Tawnisha and nearly dropped her makeup brush.

"My God, Tawni! Kinky Cat Woman?"

When she looked closer, she *did* drop her jaw—all the way to the floor beneath her own four-inch crystal-clear heels. Why she continued to be surprised by her friend's outrageous outfits she'd never know. Vera had worked at the club for nearly four years now and Tawni's daring outfits still managed to shock her. Tawni always teased her for being too naive for an exotic dancer. Maybe she was right.

"Too much?" her friend asked.

Vera choked on a laugh. "Uh. Maybe too *little?*" Yikes. "Aren't there parts missing?" The black latex Cat Woman costume—complete with whip—was minus several strategic bits. The outfit left pretty much nothing to the imagination.

But then again, Vera reminded herself, that was the whole idea here, wasn't it?

Tawni grinned. "Only the important parts."

"Too hot to handle, girl!"

"Just the reaction I'm going for." Tawni wiggled her hips in imitation of what she'd be doing onstage in a few minutes. "Rumor is there's a real hottie out there tonight."

Vera grinned. "Loaded, too, I hope? Because I could seriously use a few good tips tonight."

"You and me both." Tawni crooked her fingers playfully. "Come to mama, baby. Let's see you boys flash those twenty-dollar bills."

"Twenties? Damn. That outfit's gonna bring out the *fifties*."

"What I like to hear, girlfriend," Tawni said. "Those poor slobs don't stand a chance." She gave the mirror a final check, winked and strutted out of the dressing room.

Ho-kay, then. Great news for Tawni. Bad news for Vera. If the punters tossed all their cash at the Kinky Cat Woman during the first set, there'd be nothing left for Vera's Naughty Bride half an hour later. No, not good. Joe's retirement home payment was due in a few days, and after her vintage Camry finally broke down last week she was still three hundred bucks short, let alone her own expenses for the month.

Unbidden, her eyes suddenly swam at the thought of her once-burly stepfather lying in his antiseptic white room. He'd been so full of life, had so many friends, before. Now…she was his only visitor, and he hadn't even recognized her two nights ago.

She blew out a breath, fanning her misty eyes. *Don't go all weepy on me, Mancuso. Spoil your makeup and forget about those big tips. Buck up, girl!*

Besides, tears wouldn't help—they never did.

And if she got really desperate, she could always borrow the money from Darla, her sister. Well, half sister. Except Darla had taken off, and who knew when she'd be back. Maybe Tawni could help out if worse came to worst. *If* her friend hadn't already spent all her money on some outrageous new costume by that time. The woman went through expensive stage outfits like Vera went through romance novels.

Not that Vera should be complaining about the costumes. In fact, she was very grateful for them. Tawni was one of the big reasons the punters kept coming back night after night— and telling their friends back home in Des Moines about the great club they'd found in Vegas on their last business trip. *Diamond Lounge: Women in the rough, perfect and polished.* Yeah, that's what it actually said on the playbill out front. Seriously. With a sigh, Vera rolled her eyes. Lecherous Lou's idea, of course. Who else? Now *there* was a loser. Why couldn't *he* get Alzheimer's and forget all about Vera and his relentless campaign to get her to sleep with him?

Anyway, Tawni was one of the rough girls. Supposedly, according to Lecherous Lou. And Vera was polished. She snorted. Ha. Tawnisha Adams had graduated from UCLA magna cum laude and was one of the smoothest operators she knew. *Vera* was the only trailer trash around here, living the life her mother had lived before her. Mentally kicking and silently screaming.

Ah, well. It was what it was.

She leaned forward toward the big lighted mirror that covered an entire wall of the dressing room and critically examined her already generous eye makeup. Maybe a bit more mascara.

There was a fine line between virgin and whore. In her act, she was supposed to be a blushing, innocent bride who revealed her inner bad girl on her wedding night. Right. Like a *real* virgin would ever know those moves she did onstage. Hell, *she* barely did. But whatever. The punters loved it. Which kept Lecherous Lou from firing her even though she steadfastly refused to "do the dirty" with him, as he disgustingly referred to it. That's all that really mattered. Keeping her job.

At least until her Prince Charming came to sweep her away from all of this. Maybe tonight would be the night.

Uh-huh.

She sighed. More mascara it was.

"Vera!"

Her sister burst through the dressing-room door and skidded to a halt against the vanity counter, scattering bottles of nail polish and hair products willy-nilly.

Darla's expression was wild. "Thank God you're here!"

"Whoa!" Vera jumped up and steadied her. "Sis, what's wrong? Where have you *been* all week? You have to stop disappearing like that. Tell me what's going on!"

"Trust me, you don't want to know," Darla said, yanking open her purse.

Darla'd done one of her runners two weeks ago. Which in itself wasn't unusual. Her ditzy sister took off for parts unknown all the time, at the drop of a hat. But she always came back happier and even more relaxed than she normally was, never looking like hell warmed over. Or agitated.

Like this.

"Darla, you look something the cat dragged in," Vera said, genuine worry starting to hum through her. "Seriously, are you all right?" She'd never seen her chronically anesthetized and laid-back half sister so upset. Well, not since their poor excuse for a father had tried to throw Vera out of Darla's penthouse apartment for being a, quote, "money-grubbing gold-digging daughter of a streetwalker." But that was a whole different story.

"Yes. *No!* Oh, I don't know," Darla wailed. "Where the hell *is* it?" Stuff spilled all over the dressing table as she clawed desperately through her designer purse. A new Kate Spade, Vera noted. The real deal. Not like the knockoff Vera was carrying today, sitting on the counter next to Darla's purse. What a difference.

She caught a lipstick that went flying. "Sis, you're talking crazy. Where's *what?*"

"I gotta get out of town for a while, Vera. And I need you to do something for me— Yes! Here it is!"

Triumphantly, her sister held up a ring. A big sparkly one. Jeez Louise, was that a *diamond?* Nah, had to be fake. Even rich-as-Ivanka-Trump Darla St. Giles wouldn't have a rock that huge.

Daria thrust the ring at her. "Can you hide this for me back at our place somewhere?"

Despite their father's objections, Vera shared Darla's penthouse apartment, for which—at Darla's insistence—she paid a ridiculously small amount of rent. Amazingly generous, and a true godsend. Without it Vera'd be living in some low-rent dive in the burbs, an hour from work. Or on a sidewalk grate.

Half sisters, Vera was a product of their playboy father Maximillian St. Giles's legendary philandering. It pleased Darla—whom he basically ignored in favor of her older brother—Henry—to no end to throw their father's many faults and mistakes in his face. Sharing a penthouse with his by-blow ranked right up there. Why should Vera feel guilty about that? The man had treated them both like crap. And it was fun having a sister, even if Darla was a bit out of control at times. Okay, most of the time. They even looked alike. Superficially, at least. Darla meant a lot to her. She'd do anything for her sister.

She looked at the diamond ring in her hand. "Omigod, it's

gorgeous! Where'd you get it? Why do you want me to hide it?" Vera asked, instantly drawn in by the astoundingly beautiful sparkling jewel.

Darla scooped her stuff back into her Kate Spade. "Just as a favor. Lord, you're a lifesaver. I—" Her sister turned and for the first time noticed what Vera was wearing. Her eyes widened and a fleeting grin passed over her lips. "Dang, sis. *Great* corset. Man, that'll have 'em whackin' off in the aisles."

Darla always did have a way with words.

"Thanks, I think," Vera said wryly. Another thing about Darla: she might be an unholy mess, but she was an honest and genuine unholy mess—and never, ever judged Vera. About *anything.* "It is pretty spectacular, isn't it? I had it made to match my bride costume. What do you think? I designed it myself."

Seeing the fake wedding dress hanging from the mirror, a lightbulb went off behind eyes that looked so much like Vera's own. "Oh, it's fabulous," Darla exclaimed. "Hey! The ring'll blend right in! Go ahead, put it on," she urged.

She didn't have to ask twice. Vera slid the flashy ring onto her finger. "Wow. A perfect fit. It is so incredibly beautiful." And Darla was right. It went great with the bride outfit.

Again Vera's eyes were dazzled by the kaleidoscope of colors swirling in its center—green and blue and violet. Like one of those pinwheel whirly things used to hypnotize people in bad movies.

She shook her head to clear it of the weird feeling. "Seriously, what's the deal with the ring?"

A noise sounded out in the hall. Her sister darted a panicked glance at the door, then gave her a smile she knew darn well was forced. "No deal," Darla said. "Just hide it for me, okay?"

"Okay, but—"

"And whatever you do, do *not* talk to Thomas."

As in Thomas Smythe? Darla's ex-boyfriend? Before Vera could ask anything more, Darla pulled her into a quick, hard hug, then grabbed her Kate Spade and vanished out the door as quickly as she'd arrived.

Okay, *that* couldn't be good. Something was up.

Darla was *never* like that—all twitchy and in a rush. Darla never rushed anywhere. Or panicked over anything. Possibly because of the drugs she used far more than she should, but no doubt also because she had learned long ago that money could solve anything and everything. Even a messed-up life.

Tell her about it. Vera only wished *she'd* had the chance to learn that particular lesson.

Speaking of which, she'd better get her butt moving. If she missed her cue to go onstage, Lecherous Lou would pitch a fit. And have one more excuse to hit on her and expect capitulation. Gak. As if.

Luckily, because of her close association with the wealthy St. Giles family, Lecherous Lou—along with everyone else at the Diamond Lounge—was under the mistaken impression that Vera was loaded, too, and didn't need this job. That she just played at exotic dancing as a lark, to piss off conservative parents or whatever. Thank God for small favors. She knew other girls at the club didn't have that kind of leverage against Lecherous Lou to resist his overtures. Or other, shadier propositions. She'd heard about the "private gentlemen's parties" he ran off the books. It was really good money, and she'd been sorely tempted a time or two, but in the end, the thought of what else she'd be expected to do—according to those who did—made her just plain queasy. She shuddered with revulsion.

She might really, *really* need this job…and she might not have had sex in so long she'd probably forgotten how to do it…but she would never, ever, *ever*—

No. Way.

Hell, she wouldn't even do lap dances.

Brushing off the sordid feeling, she carefully shook out the satin skirt of her faux wedding dress and wrapped it around her waist, fastening it over the sexy white, beribboned corset she was wearing. Then she slid on the matching satin bolero-style jacket that made her look oh, so prim and proper, just like a blushing bride. Gathering the yards and yards of see-through veil—the punters particularly liked when she teased them with that—she attached the gossamer cloud to a glittering rhinestone tiara that held it in place on her head.

There.

She checked herself in the mirror. Not bad. The dress was actually gorgeous. In it, she felt like Cinderella stepping from the pumpkin coach. Every man's fantasy bride come to life.

For a split second, a wave of wistfulness sifted through her at the sight of her own reflection. Too bad it was all just an illusion.

She sighed. Oh, well. Maybe someday it would happen for real.

Sure. Like right after Las Vegas got three feet of snow in July.

Face it, Prince Charming was never going to sweep her off her feet and marry her. Who was she kidding? She knew when she got into this gig that no man she'd ever want to marry would look twice at her in that way again. Not after he found out where she came from, and on top of that, what she did for a living. It didn't matter that she'd graduated high school at the top of her class and could have gotten a full ride to any college—even Stanford. Wouldas and couldas didn't matter to men. Only perceptions. She knew that. Look what had happened to her own mother, a woman as smart and loving as any who'd ever lived, bless her.

She knew it would kill Mama, absolutely eviscerate her, if she were alive to see what Vera was doing.

But what choice did she have?

A mere high school graduate could not find an honest, decent job that paid enough to keep Joe in that pricey retirement home. And she'd be damned if she let the best man she'd ever met waste away his last years parked at some damn trailer park day care because she couldn't afford to pay for a proper assisted-living facility. No sirree. Never. Not as long as Vera had breath in her body. And boobs and an ass that could attract fifty-dollar bills. Heck, even the occasional hundred.

So. Off she went to the stage. And truth be told, she didn't even mind that much. Honestly. She *liked* her body. She'd been born with generous curves, and it did not bother her a bit to use them to her advantage. She'd never been shy. And if looking at her nude body could bring a few moments of pleasure to some lonely businessman jonesing for his far-off wife or girlfriend, well, hallelujah. Maybe she'd saved their marriage. Because men could look all they wanted, but they could not touch. That was a firm and fast rule. Both for the club and her personally.

"Two minutes!" Jerry, the bored UNLV senior and part-time stagehand, called from the hallway.

Pursing her bright red lips, she blew a good-luck kiss to the framed photo of Joe and Mama that sat at her spot on the dressing-room vanity, then hurried out and up the stairs toward the black-curtained wings of the stage. Tawni was just coming off.

"How's the house tonight?" Vera whispered.

Smiling broadly, Tawni shook a thick bundle of green bills in her fist. "Hot, baby, hot. Some real high rollers tonight. And, oh, those rumors were true. There's one singularly fine-lookin' man out there. You go get 'em, girl. Knock their little you-know-whats off."

Vera giggled. "You are *so* bad."

Tawni waggled her eyebrows and snapped her Cat Woman whip so it cracked the air. "And lovin' every minute." She raised a considering brow. "Though, Mr. Handsome didn't pay me no nevermind, so maybe he's ripe for a more frilly feminine type."

"One can only hope." *And* that he was rich as Croesus.

"Ten seconds, Miss LaRue." That came from Jerry.

Tawni gave her a wink, and Vera stepped up to the curtain.

"And now, gentlemen—" Lecherous Lou's smarmy, fake-Scottish accent crooned over the club PA system. Her music cued up with a long note from a church organ. "—you are in for a verra special treat, indeed. This next lass is guaranteed to make all you confirmed bachelors out there want to slip a gold ring on her finger and take her home for your verra own fantasy wedding night."

Stifling a yawn, Jerry stood with his nose buried in a textbook, curtain in hand, timing her entrance to exactly when the applause and male howling peaked. He didn't even look up. She didn't take it personally. Jerry'd just come out of the closet. Besides, he had exams this week.

"The Diamond Lounge is verra proud to present…"

She took a deep breath. The stage went black.

Showtime.

"Miss Vera LaRue!"

Chapter 2

Defense attorney Darius "Conner" Rothchild couldn't believe his luck.

What were the chances he'd go out on a little fishing expedition for the Parker case and end up running into Darla St. Giles, the very woman he'd been trying to track down for two weeks? At a strip joint, of all places…called, of all things, the Diamond Lounge.

The superb irony of the name did not escape him. Nor did the amazing coincidence of running into her there. Normally, Conner didn't believe in coincidences. But this just might be the genuine article.

Peeling a twenty from the roll of various bills he always carried in his pants pocket, he paid for another beer and scanned the dark club again.

Talk about two birds with one stone.

Being a Rothchild, a full partner in the family law firm of

Rothchild, Rothchild and Bennigan, and independently wealthy, all allowed him to take on a number of pro bono cases in between his paying clients. The Suzie Parker case was one of his current charity projects—a sordid affair concerning organized prostitution, unlawful coercion and sexual harassment. Several club managers on the Strip had gotten it into their minds to make their more desperate dancers attend infamous "gentlemen's house parties." Nothing more than sex parties. The girls were made to do disgusting things, often against their will, according to Suzie Parker. Unfortunately, the same reasons that led them into the coercion kept them from talking to Conner. And if he couldn't prove Suzie was telling the truth, she'd go to jail for prostitution, and her abusers would go scot-free.

But Darla St. Giles had nothing to do with the Parker case.

No. *She* was going to tell him what had happened to the missing Rothchild family heirloom, the Tears of the Quetzal, a unique chameleon diamond ring worth millions. She'd tell him, or he'd personally wring her spoiled-little-rich-girl neck. Or better yet, have her tossed into jail where *she* belonged.

He just had to find her first. Where had she disappeared to?

As Conner made a second circuit of the club looking for her, his mind raced over the facts of this case. Going into the Las Vegas Metropolitan Police Department headquarters last week, he'd literally run into Darla, one of two heirs to Maximillian St. Giles's billion-dollar fortune. Though they'd met many times socially because their families ran in the same lofty circles, Darla hadn't given Conner a second glance. She'd been too busy arguing with a cop on the sidewalk across the street from Metro headquarters. The pair of them had sounded like they were furious at each other, lost to the world in the throes of their disagreement. There'd also been something about the cop, Conner remembered thinking, something that didn't quite fit—other than his disgusting cheap cologne—although Conner hadn't been able to put his finger on it.

At the time he'd dismissed the incident as one of Darla's notorious public tantrums and continued on the errand his uncle Harold had sent him on: attempting to retrieve the Tears of the Quetzal diamond from police custody. The priceless ring was being held by LVMPD as material evidence in a high-profile murder trial—the victim being Conner's own cousin Candace Rothchild.

Her murder had hit the whole family hard, especially Conner's uncle. Hard enough to make Harold set aside a lifelong animosity and deliberate distancing of himself from all things connected with his rival brother—including his two nephews—in order to beg Conner for a favor. Get back the ring, or Harold was absolutely convinced terrible things would befall *everyone* in the family, due to some ancient curse connected with the ring. His daughter Candace had apparently been killed when she, against her father's strict orders, had "borrowed" the ring and worn it to a star-studded charity function at one of the big new casinos. She was just the first to die, Harold had warned. The man seemed genuinely terrified, convinced the so-called curse was real. He had become obsessed over retrieving the ring…especially after the near-fatal accident that befell his other daughter, Conner's cousin Silver, a few weeks back. An accident her new fiancé, AD, now suspected was a murder attempt.

Conner didn't believe in curses, but he did believe in family. He had a good relationship with his own parents and brother, but relations with Harold and his various offspring, Conner's cousins, had been more than strained for as long as he could remember.

Growing up, the deceased Candace and her coven of siblings and half siblings—Natalie, Candace's twin, who was now a Metro detective; Silver, the former pop star who'd recently made a stunning comeback; Jenna, the Vegas event planner; and the newest addition, Ricky, the devil child—every one of them used to bait him mercilessly about being born into the "wrong" side of the Rothchild family. Conner's highly respected attorney father, Michael Rothchild, was worth millions, but not billions like casino magnate Uncle Harold. Of course, that side of the family didn't even get along with each other, especially tabloid-diva Candace. Things had only gotten worse when she'd married and divorced a drunken loser drummer in a would-be rock band, leaving two beautiful but very neglected children in the constant care of nannies.

Wasn't family wonderful.

But to everyone's credit, things had changed dramatically after Candace's murder. Olive branches had been extended. Although, to be honest, he'd been reconciled with his cousins Natalie and Silver for a while now. They'd actually become good friends over the past few years…much to the chagrin of Uncle Harold. But he had changed now. And this was Conner's big chance to help bring the whole Rothchild family—imperfect as it was—back together. He did not intend to blow it.

Which was why he'd agreed to try to retrieve the ring from the police. Technically, the Tears of the Quetzal belonged to the entire family, having been unearthed in the Rothchild's Mexican diamond mine by his grandfather over five decades ago. But Uncle Harold had always been the ring's caretaker. And now with the ring's disappearance, he was obsessively worried it would bring danger to the family.

Although Conner still dismissed the ridiculous notion of curses, he did agree the diamond was not secure, even surrounded by hundreds of cops. As a lawyer, Conner knew firsthand that evidence disappeared from police custody all the time. Lost. Tampered with. Deliberately "misplaced."

And wouldn't you know it. Two weeks ago when he'd gotten to the evidence room, minutes after running into Darla St. Giles, he'd discovered, to his frustration, the unique and unmistakable chameleon diamond ring had vanished. Switched. Replaced with a paste copy that had gone missing from Harold's current wife's jewelry box. At Metro police headquarters, the theft had been pulled off by a cop who had apparently simply walked in and checked the real ring out of the evidence room on the pretense of having it examined for DNA, and left the clever fake in its place when he returned it an hour later.

Conner had gone ballistic. What was *wrong* with these people? Didn't they check ID? His cousin Natalie, the LVMPD detective, had led the search.

Then he'd remembered Darla arguing outside with that not-quite-right cop only ten minutes before he'd discovered the theft. And *that's* when he'd figured out what was wrong with the guy. His boots. They'd been brown and scuffed up. Regulation was black and spit-polished.

Conner was absolutely convinced that phony cop and Darla St. Giles were responsible for the theft of the ring from police headquarters. Damned unexpected, but not outside the realm of possibility. According to the tabloids, Darla had been scraping the proverbial bottom of the barrel of late, friend-wise and behavior-wise. Dating fake cops, stealing jewelry and hanging out at strip clubs would be right up her alley.

The question was, was the pair also involved in his cousin Candace's murder? He couldn't believe it of Darla. She was a wild party girl and definitely sliding down a slippery slope. A thief, yes. But a murderer? He could be wrong, but he didn't buy it. Still, he owed it to the family to find out for sure.

Naturally, after Conner raised the alarm, by the time Natalie had launched a search, Darla and the man had been long gone. Just in case, Conner had spent hours on the computer with Natalie by his side, looking at photos of every single police officer in Las Vegas. The man he'd seen was not among them. Therefore his instincts had been right—the culprit was not a real cop.

On that same day Darla had dropped out of sight completely, confirming his suspicions of her guilt. Despite Natalie assigning an officer to stake out her penthouse apartment 24/7, other than a single roommate, no one had seen hide nor hair of her there, or anywhere else, since.

Until now.

At least, ten minutes ago… But he'd lost her.

With mounting frustration, Conner had searched the Diamond Lounge from top to bottom for the illusive Darla. Twice. And come up empty.

Where the hell was she?

"Can I get you something, doll?" one of the waitresses asked him with a sultry smile. She was pretty. Blond. And topless.

Hello.

He glanced around, catapulted back to the present by the sight of so much skin. Whoa. Where had his famous powers of observation vanished to?

The Diamond Lounge was an Old Las Vegas landmark, a throwback to the times when total nudity was permitted along with serving alcohol. Naturally, he'd vaguely noticed the naked woman dancing on the stage. But how could he have been so angry and distracted that he hadn't noticed the all but naked women prancing around him carrying trays of drinks?

"You looking for someone special?" she asked, her smile growing even more suggestive.

Oy. He slashed a hand through his hair, composing himself. One always learned more playing nice than coming off like a demanding nutcase. And, hell, she was hot. No hardship there.

He smiled back. "Yeah. I thought I saw a friend of mine. Darla St. Giles. You know her by any chance?"

"Oh, sure," the waitress said, interest perking. He could practically see dollar signs flashing in her baby blues. As one of the rich and reckless, Darla's male friends were sure to be rich and reckless, too. Emphasis on the rich part. "She's in here all the time."

Popular landmark or not, that surprised him. "She is?"

"Uh-huh. To visit her sister. She works here."

He-llo. A St. Giles? Working at the Diamond Lounge as a topless waitress? Hell's bells. Ol' Maximillian St. Giles must be spitting disco balls over that one. Except now that Conner thought about it, he had never heard of a second St. Giles sister. There was a brother, Henry, but not... Unless... He tipped his head. "Are you *sure* they're sisters?"

"*Half* sisters, if you know what I mean. Although that's all hush-hush." The waitress waggled her eyebrows and leaned against the bar, folding her arms under her bare breasts so they pushed up toward him. Oh. Subtle. "Guess she likes walkin' on the wild side, or somethin'."

Or something. Whoa. All Conner's stress just oozed out of him. A deep, dark St. Giles secret, eh? A secret so hidden that Darla felt safe coming here tonight, even when she hadn't been to her apartment in two weeks and hadn't called her own family. Hell, all he had to do was put a watch on the secret sister and sooner or later Darla'd turn up here.

The Tears of the Quetzal was as good as found. And Natalie could bring her in for questioning about Candace's murder as well.

Damn, he was good.

"How 'bout you, doll?" the waitress asked, interrupting his thoughts again.

"Me, what?" he asked.

"You like walkin' on the wild side?"

He smiled at her. "Maybe." Then took a second look at what the blond waitress was offering up. He was used to women throwing themselves at him, one of the perks of his looks and his famous last name. Normally he was just too damn busy to take advantage. But what the hell, it had been a long time; maybe the Parker case could wait another night. But first… "Darla's sister, she around?" Just so he'd know who to look for. Tomorrow.

"Sure, she's coming on right now. That's her." The waitress pointed toward the stage.

The stage? He tore his eyes from her and turned. "You mean she's a—"

He froze, literally, instantly oblivious to everything else around him.

The sister… At first Conner thought it was Darla; they looked so much alike. But then she stepped into the spotlight, and all resemblance vanished. The woman was the most amazingly, lusciously gorgeous thing he'd ever seen in his life. She glided out on the horseshoe-shaped stage to the tune of Mendelssohn's *Wedding March*. Eyes cast demurely down, she was dressed in a frothy, whipped-cream wedding dress, complete with a long poofy veil covering her face and spilling over her shoulders and back clear to the floor like some kind of gossamer waterfall.

Wow.

Normally, the merest glimpse of a wedding dress made him break out in hives and sprint hell-bent-for-leather in the opposite direction. Not this one.

"Her?" he asked the waitress, totally forgetting that just seconds ago he'd been contemplating—

Never mind. What waitress?

Was he actually hyperventilating?

"Yeah. How about we—"

"What's her name?" he asked, his eyes completely glued to the perfect vision onstage.

The waitress was not pleased. He could tell by the way she huffed and turned her back on him. Working on autopilot, he dug out his ubiquitous roll, peeled off a bill and held it over his shoulder for her. "Her name?"

She gave a harrumph and snatched it. "It's Vera. Vera LaRue."

Vera… Wait. Wasn't that the name Natalie had said belonged to Darla's roommate? The *sister* was the roommate?

The churchy organ music morphed into a slow, grinding striptease number. Conner watched, beguiled, as Vera LaRue slowly started to move her body in a sinuous dance. And, damn, could the woman ever move her body. Her eyes were still cast innocently at the floor doing her vestal virgin bit, but there wasn't a man in the place watching her face.

Conner pushed off the bar and signaled a passing waitress, peeling off another few bills. Without saying a word, he was shown to a table, front and center. He sat down, and a glass of champagne appeared in his hand. Vera paused just above him on the stage. Oh. Man. She was close enough to touch. He was more than tempted to try.

She raised her lashes and looked down at him.

He looked up at her.

Their eyes met.

And sweet holy God. He was struck by lightning.

Or maybe just blinded by the flash of seven carats of chameleon diamond on her finger as she slowly unbuttoned the top of her gown. He almost fell off his chair. That was *his* seven carats of chameleon diamond! She was wearing the Tears of the Quetzal!

Well, hot damn. If this was Harold's so-called danger, bring it on.

The top of the white gown slid provocatively off Vera

LaRue's pale, pretty shoulders. Conner watched her slowly tug the sleeves down her arms, inch by tantalizing inch. For several moments his brain ceased to function.

Until he gave himself a firm mental kick. What was *wrong* with him?

She couldn't be nearly as innocent as she appeared, clutching the top of that dazzling white gown to her breasts like a blushing virgin. Hell, she *must* be involved with Darla in the theft of the ring. The evidence was right on her finger!

Logic told him she had to be innocent of involvement in Candace's murder. Only a complete, brainless idiot would kill someone, or even be remotely connected to a murder, and then flash the evidence in front of a room full of people. Obviously, she couldn't know of the link between Candace's murder and the ring she was wearing.

Come to think of it, maybe she didn't even know the ring was stolen. Now, *that* would make more sense. It could easily be she was just being used. Or set up.

In which case, he had to give Darla props. Hiding the unique ring in plain sight, as part of her sister's stage costume, was brilliant.

Too bad he was even more brilliant.

Brilliant and ruthless.

And did he mention intrigued as hell? Who *was* this Vera LaRue, Darla St. Giles's gorgeous, secret, illegitimate half sister?

And who'd have ever thought Conner Rothchild would be so captivated by a stripper? His snooty family would have a cow, every last one of them. Especially his dad, who'd always held Uncle Harold in contempt for his questionable taste in multiple women.

But thoughts of family vanished as Vera LaRue stopped in front of him and slanted him another shy glance. She held his gaze with a sexy look as she pulled at the waist of her wedding gown and the whole thing slid down around her trim ankles in a pool of liquid silk.

For a second he couldn't breathe. Sweet merciful heaven. All that was left was the most erotic, alluring bit of lace he had ever seen grace a woman's body. Parts of it, anyway. And a veil. Straight out of Salome.

Please don't let me be drooling.

Then, with a sultry lowering of her eyelashes, she scooped up the dress and let it fall provocatively right into his lap. Her eyebrow lifted almost imperceptibly.

Okay, seriously wow. A challenge? Clearly, she did not know him. Conner didn't lose. And if there was one thing he never lost, it was a dare.

Oh. Yeah.

He looked up at her and conjured his most seductive smile.

Still moving to the music, she knelt down on the stage. Right before him. With those melting eyes and amazing mile-long legs…encased in white thigh-high stockings and impossibly sexy crystal-clear high-heeled shoes. She dropped to her hands and knees. Just for him.

His brain pretty much disintegrated. The rest of his body was set to explode. He was hard and thick as one of those columns at the Forum. The *real* one in Rome.

The Rothchild heirloom flashed on her finger. His family's ring. A smile curved his lips.

She wanted his family jewel? Well, then. He just might have to be a gentleman and give it to her.

Oh, yes. This curse could prove to be very, very interesting, indeed.

Chapter 3

The applause for Vera LaRue was deafening. Conner watched mesmerized as she took her final bow and swished off the stage.

He let out a long, long breath. Lord, have *mercy.*

By the time she'd finished her incredible dance of temptation, she'd made her way all around the stage, weaving her erotic spell over the dozens of men who were pressed up to the edge like pathetic dogs panting for a treat. But Conner was the only one who'd rated personal attention from her. It was like she'd danced for him alone, even when she was all the way across the stage. Of course, probably every guy there thought exactly the same thing. That's what a good stripper did to a guy. Or maybe she singled him out because he was the only one who hadn't attempted to put his hands on her. Hadn't tipped her. Hadn't done anything but hold her sultry eyes with his and silently promise her anything she wanted. Anything at all.

On his terms.

She'd ended up gloriously, unabashedly naked. Or, as good as. Down to a G-string, stockings and those take-me heels…and the Quetzal diamond. Oh, yeah, and a thick layer of fluttering greenbacks stuck into her G-string, making it look like a Polynesian skirt gone triple X.

Her bridal veil was around Conner's neck. He was still sweating over the way she'd put it there.

Da-*amn*. The woman was Salome incarnate. But Conner fully intended to have her dancing to *his* tune before the night was over. Singing like a lark about how she'd ended up with his ring on her finger…without even benefit of dinner and a movie. Not to mention if she knew anything about Candace's death.

Conner was a damn good lawyer, skilled at making witnesses trust him enough to spill their guts. It was all about the approach. So…how to best approach this one…?

He looked around the room. And almost laughed out loud. The answer was beckoning from the back of the club. Aw, gee. He'd just have to sacrifice himself.

Throwing back the last of his champagne—not that he needed the Dutch courage—he signaled his waitress.

"I'd like Miss LaRue to join me," he told her as the fickle crowd roared for the new cutie who'd just come out onstage.

The waitress took the dress and veil from him. "Sure, hon. I'll have her come to your table."

He pulled off another bill. "No, somewhere private."

"Oh, sorry. I'm afraid Ms. LaRue doesn't do that."

"Do what?"

"Private parties. She's strictly a stage dancer."

"Really."

Now, *that* was interesting. Apparently being a St. Giles let her pick and choose her jobs. Normally the private VIP rooms upstairs were where the big money was made by these women.

And the big thrills. Personally, he'd never gotten into the whole lap dance thing. A nice sensual session in the privacy of your own home with a woman you knew and liked, sure. But an anonymous grind for cash? A bit sleazy if you asked him.

"Well," he told the waitress, "then it's good I only want to talk to her."

She rolled her eyes. "Sure you do, hon."

He could understand her skepticism. Hell, *he* was skeptical, and he knew he only wanted to talk to her. Honest.

He peeled off a few more bills and pressed them into her palm. "Tell Miss LaRue I have information about her sister. And that I'll match whatever she just made onstage."

Where she'd practically seduced him, by the way. But the woman didn't do lap dances. Something didn't add up about *that* picture.

The waitress shrugged. "You're wasting your time. Don't say I didn't warn you." She beckoned him with a crooked finger.

He strolled along behind her to the back of the club and followed her up the red-carpeted stairs to the second floor, where the inevitable small, "private entertainment" VIP rooms were located. Though gentlemen's clubs weren't Conner's favorite hangouts, one couldn't be a defense attorney in Vegas without doing a certain amount of business in them. Especially since his frequent pro bono work tended to involve hookers and runaways. So he was fairly familiar with the standard club setup.

Because of its enduring fame, Old Vegas reputation and pricey cover charge—and thanks to a complete renovation in the nineties—the Diamond Lounge wasn't too bad, compared to most. Clean. Sophisticated decor. Unobtrusive bouncers. Nice-looking, classy ladies. He supposed if you had to work in a place like this, the Diamond Lounge was definitely top drawer.

But once again he wondered why über-conservative Maximillian St. Giles let his daughter work at all, let alone take off her clothes for money. Even if she was illegitimate, and as far as he knew, unacknowledged, a negative reflection was still cast on the family.

Not that Conner was objecting to her taking off her clothes. Hell, no. The woman had an incredible body.

She also had his family's ring.

He wanted it back. That was his primary objective here. And nailing down Darla's involvement in his cousin's murder. Not nailing Vera LaRue. But if in the course of things, he ended up close and personal with her, well, who was he to protest? Especially considering the unmistakable signals she'd given him from up onstage. She had to be expecting this.

Handing the waitress his credit card, he did a quick survey of the tiny, soundproof room, then sprawled onto the heavy, red leather divan that took up most of one wall. Soft music played in the background. Scented candles littered the surfaces of two low tables at either end of the divan, as well as on the heavy wood mantel of the fireplace across from it. The tasteful cornice lighting was recessed and rose-colored, lending a pastel glow to Oriental rugs over cream-colored carpet and gauzy curtains that looked more like mosquito nets draped all around the walls of the room. It was like being cocooned in some exotic Caribbean bordello.

Oddly arousing.

The curtains over the door parted, and Vera LaRue suddenly stood there, holding a sweating champagne bottle and two crystal flutes. She'd put the wedding dress back on.

Hey, now.

"Hello," she said, her voice throaty and rich like a tenor sax. "I understand you wanted to speak with me about my sister."

Suddenly, talk wasn't at all what he wanted.

Wait. Yes, it was.

"Why don't you come in and open up that bottle," he suggested, indicating the champagne in her hand. The hand with the Tears of the Quetzal diamond on it. *Focus, Conner.*

"I, um…" She suddenly looked uncomfortable. "I'm sorry, sir. I really don't think so. Truth is, I don't do this."

He hiked a brow. "Drink champagne?"

She blinked. Flicked her gaze down to the bottle then back to him, even more flustered. "No. I mean yes, I drink champagne. Of course I drink champagne. Everyone does. But I *don't* do lap dances. I only came because you mentioned my sister. Now, what was it—"

"I understand," he cut in agreeably. Not having to endure her gyrating on his lap without being able to touch her was probably a good thing. If maybe a little disappointing. Fine, a lot disappointing. "Let's have some bubbly and then we can talk."

She gave him a look. What? She didn't believe him, either? "Sir, I'm serious. It's nothing to do with you. You seem like a nice guy. I just really don't—"

"Please. Call me Conner. If you don't want to dance for me, Ms. LaRue, that's fine. As appealing as that might be, it's not why I'm here." He held out his hand with a smile. "Here. I'll open it."

When she still balked, he stood up. That made her jump. But she recovered quickly. She gave him the bottle and pulled back her hand a little too fast. As though she were…afraid to touch him?

Impossible. The woman who'd practically had sex with him with her eyes from the stage could not possibly be nervous about physical contact, regardless of what he might or might not have had in mind for this tête à tête.

Which was *just* to talk.

Honest to God.

Or…did she perhaps realize who he was? *That* hadn't occurred to him. Had Darla warned Vera someone might come looking for the ring? Maybe asking questions about a murder? Was this modesty thing all a big ploy to throw him off?

Nah. If so, she would have run away, not flirted mercilessly and then locked herself and the ring in a tiny room with him.

The cork flew, startling her into raising the flutes to catch the golden liquid. Her satiny gown rustled against his legs as he stepped closer to fill the glasses. The scent of her perfume clung to the air around her—sweet and spicy. Very nice.

Suddenly, the most insanely irrational thought struck him. What if she really *were* his beautiful bride, that this really was their wedding night and he really *was* about to peel that bridal gown off her and—

Whoa, there, buddy. Hold on.

Where the hell had *that* come from?

Totally inappropriate temporary insanity, that was where. Obviously he'd gone without sex for *far* too long, and it was somehow damaging his brain's ability to function in the presence of a beautiful woman.

He eased a flute from her stiff fingers and clicked it with hers. Back to business.

But instead of a trust-inducing get-to-know-you question, what came out of his mouth was, "You do have some amazing moves, Ms. LaRue."

To make matters worse, his rebellious gaze inched boldly down her delectable body, all of its own volition.

Help.

"Um, thanks, Conner. I appreciate your…um, appreciation. But now you really need to tell me whatever information you have about my sister, or I'll be leaving."

Damn, she looked good. And so sweetly uncomfortable, he pulled out his roll, thumbed off two C-notes, held them up, and confessed, "Okay, you were right. I *would* like to see you dance up close."

Okay, way to go, you total moron. What was *wrong* with him? This was *not* the way he conducted business.

"I knew it." She shook her head, taking a step backward, away from him. "Look, I'm really sorry, but this is not happening. I'll just go find someone else—"

An incredible thought flew through his mind as she chattered on about getting him another girl. Could this befuddling change in his self-control be the mysterious power of the ancient Mayan legend-slash-curse Uncle Harold was always talking about? The part he was obsessed with portended terrible things would befall anyone who possessed the ring with evil intentions. But the *other* part said the spirit of the Quetzal would bring any truly worthy person within its range of influence true, abiding love.

For a second he just stood there, stunned.

He-*llo?*

Had he gone completely *insane?*

Mystical powers? True love? With an exotic dancer?

He gave himself a firm mental thwack.

And smiled at her. "No, it's you I want, and the room is already paid for." By the quarter-hour, no less. He held up his money roll. "Tell me, what did you make in tips onstage? I promised to match it." *To talk,* he tried to compel his mouth to say. But the words just wouldn't come out.

She didn't even blink. "That's very nice of you, but no. Thank you. As I said—" She launched into her spiel yet again.

But he wasn't listening. It was like he was standing next to himself watching as he was being taken over by pod people. He should be taking it slow. From arm's length. Gaining her trust. Not trying to jump her bones. Certainly not until after he'd gotten his answers. And his family's ring back. He *knew* that. But she was simply too delicious to resist.

Ah, what the hell.

He surrendered to it. Changed tactics. *Her* first. Answers later. Then the ring.

Yeah, that worked.

Determined, he thumbed out several more bills, bringing her chatter to a stuttering halt. He didn't doubt for a second she'd eventually capitulate. One thing his ruthless family had taught him—*everyone* capitulated. It was all just a matter of negotiation. "Four-hundred? Five?"

She swallowed. "Really. I don't think you under—"

He started peeling and didn't stop till he reached ten. "Let's say an even thousand, shall we?"

That really shut her up. She stared at the money, then shifted her gaze to stare at him for an endless moment. "Why?" she finally asked.

Good freaking question.

Vera LaRue was so different from the type of woman he was usually attracted to…this was completely unknown territory. Sure, he frequently worked with hookers, dancers and runaways in his legal practice. *Worked.* But he was definitely not attracted to them. Never slept with them. Ever.

So what was different about this woman? What made him want *her?* And no—hell, no!—it had *nothing* to do with mystical powers or curses.

A matter of pride maybe? Conner Rothchild wasn't used to being denied. The only time he took *that* without protest was in court.

Okay, bull.

Not pride. Not some stupid Mayan curse.

But chemistry. *Sexual* chemistry. Plain and simple. He wanted her in his bed, naked and moving on top of him. She was the sexiest woman he'd met in decades. Was this rocket science?

He wanted her. A lap dance seemed like a damned good way to convince her she wanted him, too. It was a start, anyway.

"Why?" he echoed. And gave her his best winning jury smile. "Let's just say you intrigue me."

She regarded him for another endless moment, her eyes narrowing and filling with suspicion. "Who are you, anyway?"

Uh-oh.

But as luck would have it, he never got the chance to answer. Because just then the door whooshed open and the mosquito net curtains blew aside as though from a strong wind. Two men in suits strode through and halted right inside, looking so much like federal agents that just on reflex Conner was about to warn Vera to not to say a word.

One of the men stepped forward. "Miss St. Giles?"

With a frown, Vera turned to the newcomers in confusion. "What?"

Conner frowned, too, when Forward Guy spotted the Tears of the Quetzal diamond on her finger, looked grimly smug, then officiously snapped up an ID wallet. "Special Agent Lex Duncan, FBI."

Oh, come on. Seriously?

But it was Special Agent Duncan's next words that really seemed to confuse the hell out of Vera. And him, too.

"Darla St. Giles, I am hereby placing you under arrest."

Chapter 4

"You can't do that!" Vera exclaimed as an honest-to-goodness FBI agent spun her around, grabbed her wrists and snapped handcuffs onto them. "Hey! Watch the dress!" she cried. "What the heck—"

"Ms. St. Giles, you have the right to remain silent—"

"*What?* Are you kidding? I am *not*—"

"Vera," Conner, her would-be john, cut her off over the drone of the FBI agent—what was his name? Lexicon?—reciting her rights, "don't say anything. I'll take care of this."

Not only was the man annoying but he was a real buttinsky, too. "You don't understand. I'm not—"

"I know you're not," Conner cut her off again. "But obviously *they* think you are."

"Move away from the suspect, sir," her second would-be arrestor admonished her would-be lawyer briskly, with just a touch of disdain in his voice, as Agent Lexicon continued his recitation. Great. Already with the attitude.

All at once his words registered. "Suspect?" she echoed, horrified. "*Me?* I'm *not* a suspect!" she insisted, growing more frustrated by the second. And more worried. She could see a crowd gathering outside the door. If Lecherous Lou got wind of this, her butt would be fired for sure.

One thing a club in this city did not need was bad publicity of any kind. Kept the tourists away. And her boss had just been waiting for a good excuse to fire her. Mainly because she refused his disgusting advances, but also because she wouldn't get involved in that shady business he was running on the side with a few other club managers, providing high-class dancers for private parties.

"That's right. You're no mere suspect," Agent Attitude agreed. "You've been caught red-handed, sweetheart, guilty as hell. Do not pass go, do not collect two-hundred dollars." He snickered at his own lame joke.

"What do you mean, guilty? I haven't done anything!"

"Vera," Conner headed off her impending tirade, "do *not* say another word." She snapped her mouth shut in irritation as he turned to Lex Luthor. "I'm Conner Rothchild, the lady's legal counsel. She is invoking her right to silence and to an attorney."

Wait. Oh, no. Conner *what?* Did he just say his name was—

"And by the way," Conner continued, "this woman is not Darla St. Giles. So if you would kindly take off the handcuffs and let her go?"

Rothchild! As in—

Agent Lucifer whipped around and peered closer at her. "Then who is she?" he demanded.

Rothchild! Oh, no. No way, Jose. She knew the reputation that went along with the name Conner Rothchild. She'd heard plenty of horror stories from his own cousins, tabloid-diva

Candace and pop star Silver, who used to be two of Darla's best friends. Not only was Conner a sleaze-bag shark of a defense attorney according to Candace, but according to Silver he was also possibly the biggest skirt-chaser in the state.

"She's—"

Hell, no. "I'm terribly sorry, but this man is *not* my attorney," she jumped in indignantly. "And I can answer for myself, thank you very much. My name is Vera Mancuso, and Darla St. Giles is my—"

"Stop!" Conner-freaking-playboy-of-the-year-Rothchild cut her off again with an exasperated glare. "I *said* not another word! I *am* her attorney, but since she is not the person you are looking for—"

"Oh, she's the right person, all right," the Devil's agent said resolutely. He pointed an accusing finger at her left hand. "Whoever she is, she's in possession of material evidence stolen from police custody. Therefore, Vera Mancuso, is it? I am placing *you* under arrest—"

"What?" The rest of his words faded out as Agent Attitude pried the ring from her finger and dropped it into a small Ziploc bag. "Oh. My. God. I cannot believe this." Her incredulity continued to pour out of her mouth all on its own as desperate thoughts bombarded her mind even faster.

Stolen? From the police? *Oh, Darla! What have you gotten yourself into this time?* Wait a second. Darla, nothing. Heck, what had her sister gotten *her* into this time? Now Darla's request to hide the ring made perfect sense. Stolen! She could go to jail!

Despair swept over her as the FBI agents pushed her out into the main part of the club, where every single person stood and gaped in avid interest as she was led through the room in handcuffs, tripping over the bridal gown because with the restraints she couldn't hold it up to walk. Even the new girl onstage stopped gyrating and stared wide-eyed. And, damn it, there was Lecherous Lou, looking murderous as he watched her being taken away.

Great. So much for *that* job.

What would she do for money now? How would she pay for Joe's retirement home from prison? Too bad she hadn't accepted gazillionaire Conner's proposition earlier...and gotten paid up front. That thousand bucks would at least have bought her a week or two respite. Then, oh, darn, got arrested, can't do the lap dance. Sorry, no refunds.

Yeah. Like her conscience would have let her do that, even if a thousand bucks to this man was merely a night's meaningless amusement. Honesty was such a bitch.

"You have a change of clothes in your dressing room?" Mr. Persistent Attorney asked as she was herded through the club's front door. She glanced back at him. And wondered what his real agenda was. He couldn't possibly care what happened to her.

Yeah, like she couldn't guess.

Conner Rothchild was a blue-blooded playboy who made the gossip columns nearly as often as Darla and Silver and their jet-setting, hard-clubbing cronies. Always with a different woman on his arm. He probably thought slumming it with Darla St. Giles's exotic-dancer sister would be a hoot. For about five minutes. Meanwhile, she'd be outed to the world at large, and good ol' Maximillian would be furious.

"I'll grab your purse and follow you," Conner said when she deliberately didn't answer. "Don't say anything until I get there. Nothing. I mean it."

"Look," she made one last stab at reasoning with him as she was being stuffed into the back of an unmarked SUV. The white frothy wedding dress filled the entire seat, and she had to punch it down. "Please don't bother following me. You can't be my attorney. I have no money to pay your fee, and even if I did, I—"

"Don't worry about the fee," he responded with a dismissive gesture.

Uh-huh. A girl didn't need a telescope to see exactly where this was going. "And I don't pay in kind!" she yelled just before the door slammed.

He grinned at her through the window. And had the audacity to wink.

She groaned, closed her eyes and sank down in the seat. Swell. Just freaking swell. Broke. Fired. Arrested by the FBI. And pimped out to the city's most charming keg of sexual dynamite.

What the hell else could go wrong today?

Special Agent Lex Duncan was being a real pismire.

Conner folded his hands in front of himself to keep from decking the jerk. They were standing in the observation room attached to interrogation out at the FBI's main Las Vegas field station. Vera was sitting at a table on the other side of the one-way mirror, looking tired, vulnerable and all but defeated. She hadn't started crying yet, but Conner felt instinctively she was close. Very close. Duncan had been interrogating her hard for over two hours, asking the same questions again and again. He hadn't even let her change out of that sexy break-away bridal gown into the jeans and T-shirt Conner'd brought for her along with her purse from the dressing room. Pure intimidation. The bastard.

"Listen to me. She's not involved," he told Duncan for the dozenth time. He wasn't sure when he'd started being a true believer, but he was now firmly in the Vera-isn't-involved-in-the-ring-heist-*or*-Candace's-murder camp. In fact, he was pretty convinced she wasn't guilty of a damn thing, other than a crapload of bad luck.

"And you know this how?" Duncan asked, brow raised.

"It's *my* family's damn ring, and my own murdered cousin we're talking about. Not to mention possibly the same person nearly bringing down a theater scaffold on my other cousin Silver. Don't you think I want the guilty party or parties caught and fried?" he asked heatedly.

He and Candace might not have gotten along all that well, but she was still family. He'd see the killer hanged by his balls, no doubt about it. "But I want the *right* person caught and punished. Vera Mancuso is a victim of her half sister's bad judgment. Nothing more."

Duncan pushed out a breath. "Okay. Just for sake of argument, say I agree with you. My problem is, the stolen evidence was right on her finger."

"And she explained how it got there. About fifty times. I, for one, believe her story."

"So, what, I'm supposed to release her just because *you* have a damn hunch? Or more likely, have the hots for her and want to impress her with your prowess…as her attorney?"

Conner clamped his teeth. Okay, he might have the hots for Vera, but that would have ended abruptly if he'd still had the least doubt she was part of either the ring's theft or his cousin's murder. And, yeah, maybe he didn't have any real solid reason to believe that, but there you go. A man had to trust his gut instincts. Especially if he was a lawyer.

"Yeah," he said evenly. "Just release her."

Duncan started to shake his head. "No can do."

"I have an idea," Conner said, thinking fast. "We can use her. To get her sister. That's who you really want to question about the ring."

Duncan exhaled. "I'm listening."

"Darla trusts her. She gave Vera the Tears of the Quetzal for safekeeping. Believe me, she'll be back for it."

"And?"

"And when she shows up, I'll call you and you can come arrest her. You can get to the real truth. The *real* perps."

Duncan briefly considered. "Even if I went along with this, what makes you think Ms. Mancuso will let you stick around that long?"

Conner shrugged modestly. "I'm not without my charms."

The FBI agent's eyes rolled. "And yet, she keeps telling me you're *not* her lawyer. Besides, wouldn't your representing her be a conflict of interest?"

"Not if she's innocent."

And, damn, she really did look innocent sitting there in that bleak, gray interrogation room, holding back her tears by a thread. Innocent, and incredibly brave. While Duncan questioned her, Conner'd had his legal assistant do a quick workup on Vera Mancuso. Her background had been far from easy. He'd been all wrong about her relationship with her biological father, Maximillian St. Giles. The man didn't want to know her, was openly hostile to his illegitimate daughter and kept her existence deep in the closet. The scumbag.

Duncan raked a hand through his hair. "I don't know if you're aware of this, but the FBI is not in charge of your cousin's murder case. That's strictly Metro at this point."

Conner glanced at him in surprise. "Then why didn't *they* arrest Vera?"

"Because of that ring. My current investigation is a series of high-end interstate jewelry robberies for which Darla St. Giles is a prime suspect, along with a couple of her friends. Possibly even a family member," he added pointedly. "I got a tip from an informant that Darla was seen entering the Diamond Lounge, so we closed in. I thought she might be fencing some of her stolen goods. The manager there's had some illegal dealings in the past."

"So when you saw Vera wearing the Quetzal…"

"I recognized it right away. And she looks enough like Ms. St. Giles to have fooled me for a minute. I have good reason to believe Darla's gang had targeted the Rothchild diamond on the night your cousin was killed. You seeing her with that phony cop at the police station, and the ring showing up in her half sister's possession are both pretty strong evidence to connect her to the theft."

"But what about the phony cop I saw her with?" Conner said. "And didn't you say Luke Montgomery's new wife was there at the casino the night of Candace's murder, and was later stalked by someone wanting the ring?"

Duncan crossed his arms. "All true. But even if I agree with you in theory, my hands are tied. Until Darla is in custody and corroborates Ms. Mancuso's story, and Vera's alibi is checked out, I'd be insane to let the only suspect I have go free."

Conner stuck his hands in his pockets. "Okay, I see your point. Still, keeping Vera in custody is probably the best way to drive Darla so far into hiding you'll never find her. She certainly has the means to disappear for a good long time if she feels threatened."

"So what do you propose I do?"

"Let Vera out on bail. I'll pay it. Then we use her as bait, like I suggested."

Both of them turned to contemplate Vera through the mirrored window. She'd put her head down on the Formica table and buried her face in her arms. Had she finally broken down? Conner's heart squeezed in sympathy.

"If I agree to this crazy scheme," Duncan finally said, "I'd want something in return."

"Like what?" Conner asked.

"I'd want your help figuring out exactly who is part of the jewel theft ring I'm investigating. You move in the same social circles as Darla St. Giles. You go to the same parties and charity events, know the same people. I'd want you to nose around, ask questions. Narrow down my list of suspects." He turned to look Conner in the eye. "Help LVMPD figure out if your cousin's death was a jewel robbery gone bad, or something else entirely."

Conner raised his brows. "Kind of a tall order, isn't it?"

"That's the deal. Take it or leave it."

"Fine." Obviously, Vera wasn't going to get a better offer. Nor was he. "I'll take it."

Chapter 5

They were letting her go.

Vera couldn't quite believe it. But she wasn't about to question her good luck.

Right up until the devil's Agent Lex Luthor—whose name actually turned out to be Duncan—said to her as he handed over her bag of belongings, "Your attorney, Mr. Rothchild, has posted your bail and personally vouched for your whereabouts until the arraignment. As a condition of your release, you must agree to check in with him at least three times a day."

She stopped dead. "You can't be serious."

"Bear in mind you are a potential murder suspect, Ms. Mancuso," the agent said sternly. "Personally, I'm opposed to releasing you at all, but the Rothchild name wields a lot of influence—"

She handed him back her bag. "Forget it. If that's a requirement, I'll stay arrested, thanks."

The FBI guy's jaw dropped. "Excuse me?"

"No one ever listens to me. I've told you over and over, he's *not* my—"

"Actually, he is." Duncan held up a paper. "Court appointed. I have the order here if you need proof."

She blinked. Oh, for crying out loud. The man was totally relentless. "Let me see that."

It didn't matter that for some mysterious reason she found the loathsome Conner Rothchild so incredibly, toe-curlingly sexy that every time she looked at him she practically melted into a limp noodle at his feet. Or that the whole time he'd sat in the audience at the Diamond Lounge—*before* she knew who he was—she'd girlishly pretended he was the only man in the whole room, and danced for him alone. When had *that* ever happened before? With any man? Never, that's when.

But even so. She wasn't about to trade sex for lawyering. Or anything, for that matter. She knew what he must have in mind, and she wanted none of it. Well. Not like that, anyway. She probably wouldn't say no under other circumstances or if he were anyone else. But selling herself? No way. Regardless of how mouthwateringly and wrongly tempting he was. And how much she really wanted to find out what it would be like to lie under his ripped, athletic body and—

Oh, no. Banish *that* thought.

She looked over the paper that Duncan had handed her. Sure enough, it was a one-paragraph court order appointing Conner as her legal counsel.

What. Ever.

At least she didn't have to pay him. *Or* owe him in any other way. That was a huge relief.

But did she want to have to check in with Mr. Cutthroat Playboy Attorney three times a day like she was one of his low-life parolees? Heck, no.

"Have you ever been to prison, Ms. Mancuso?" the federal agent asked. Apparently mind reading was part of the FBI arsenal.

"Of course not."

"Trust me, you wouldn't enjoy it." He took back the paper and slid it into her file. "Mr. Rothchild seems like a decent attorney. Let him help you."

She regarded him. "Special Agent Duncan, if I were your little sister, would you be saying the same thing?"

He gazed back steadily. "If you were my little sister, you wouldn't be in this mess, and you sure as hell wouldn't be stripping for a living. You might think about what kind of future you want for yourself before choosing sides, Ms. Mancuso."

With that, he put her bag of belongings back in her hand, took her arm and hauled her down the hall and out into the reception area where Conner Rothchild was waiting.

Why, the arrogant bastard! She'd never been so—

"Everything okay?" Conner asked, eyeing the two of them. Vera was so mad she didn't trust herself to answer. Who knew what would come flying out of her mouth, landing her in even worse trouble?

"Just peachy," Duncan said, and unceremoniously handed her arm over to Conner, like a recalcitrant child turned over to her father for disciplining. "Make sure you know where she is at all times, Rothchild. If I were you, I wouldn't let her out of your sight."

"I'm sure we'll come to an understanding," Conner said, his face registering wary surprise.

"Just don't forget our agreement," Duncan admonished him, then without another word, he turned and stalked off.

"Okay, then," Conner said when he was gone. "What was *that* all about?"

She didn't know why she was so upset. This sort of thing

happened all the time, whenever anyone outside the business found out what she did for a living. She could call herself an exotic dancer all she liked. To everyone else she'd always be a stripper. She should be used to the disdain by now. But it still hurt every darn time.

"He doesn't approve of me," she muttered.

The lawyer frowned. "He said that?"

Some people could be so righteous and judgmental. They had no clue about the vicious cycle of poverty a woman could so easily fall into. She was one of the lucky ones who'd found a way out. Or at least a way to stay above water.

She sighed. *Get over it, girl.* "No. He said I should trust you."

"Well, you should," Conner said, brows furrowing. He glanced after the FBI agent. "Listen, if he said anything inappropriate, I'll go back in there and—"

"No, please—" She reached out to stop him…and got the shock of her life. The second she touched him, a spill of tingling pleasure coursed from her fingers—her *ring* finger to be exact—down her arm and through her torso, straight to her center.

She gasped.

He looked just as stunned.

She jerked her hand back. Too late. A flood of emotions washed through her. Not just physical desire, though God knew that came through strong and clear, but also a disconcerting mix of tenderness and trust. And…a kind of soul-deep recognition. That this man was *her* man. The man she'd been waiting for all her life. Her Prince Charming.

She swallowed heavily. Okay, so yikes. It was official. She'd totally lost her mind.

If only he'd stop staring at her like that. Like she had two heads or something.

"I'll take you home," he said abruptly.

"No," she said. "I can take a cab."

"Don't be ridiculous."

He put a hand to the small of her back and ushered her out the front entrance and into the night nearly as quickly as Duncan had dragged her through the field office's brightly lit inner corridors. Conner must have changed his mind about her, too. That was quick. Maybe that jolt knocked some sense into him. Too bad it hadn't for her. More like the opposite. He kept getting more and more attractive every minute that went by.

The shimmering heat of the Las Vegas nighttime enveloped her as she stepped into it, calming as always. It tamed the shivering in her chest and limbs. Filled her lungs with sage-scented comfort, like on long-ago evenings spent in her mama's lap in an old secondhand rocker in a tiny patch of garden behind their mobile home.

"Please," she said when they hit the parking lot. "Slow down. These shoes aren't really meant for walking in." Or maybe her knees still needed to recover from that Prince Charming nonsense.

He halted, glancing down at her four-inch-heeled glass slippers, which sparkled back at him in the reflected streetlamps.

Ah, jeez. The symbolism was just too damn perfect. She felt herself going beet red in embarrassment.

"Really, th-thanks for your assistance," she stammered, "but I'd prefer to take a cab home."

She turned toward the fenced perimeter and the street beyond and realized with a sinking feeling that taxis would be few and far between in this neighborhood, even during daylight hours. And it must be three in the morning by now. She'd have to go back inside and have them call—

Suddenly she found herself swept up in Conner's arms, her wrist looped around his neck.

"Hey! What are you doing?"

"Kick them off."

"Huh?"

"The shoes. Lose them. They're ludicrous."

"And expensive! No way!"

He made a face. "Lord, you're stubborn."

She mirrored it right back. "God, you're obnoxious."

They glared at each other for a moment.

"Fine," Conner said. "Keep the damn shoes."

"Thank you, I will. Now if you'll please put me down."

He actually snorted at her. "Can't you just accept my help gracefully?"

Before she had a chance to respond, he was carrying her toward a midnight-blue convertible sports car sitting in the first slot of the parking lot. It was the most dazzling car she'd ever seen in her life. And totally intimidating. Low, sleek, catlike in grace and Transformer-like in technology. It had to have cost more than she earned in a year. Or two. His hand moved and a couple of beeps sounded. The two car doors rose up like the wings of a giant bird.

"Holy moly. What is this, the Batmobile?"

"No, a Mercedes-Benz SLR McLaren Roadster." He lowered her into the passenger seat. She sank down into the buttery leather and it hugged her backside like a lover spooning her body. Softly firm and enveloping. "You don't like it?"

"It's, um…" Luxurious. Flashy and unreasonably sexy, like its owner. Totally out of her league. Like its owner. "Nice."

"Nice, huh?" He gave her a lopsided grin as he dropped down to sit on his heels next to her car door. He pulled the seat belt over her lap, leaned over and fought with the airy poofs of her faux wedding dress for a moment finding the socket to snap it into.

She heard the click. But his arms stayed lost in the voluminous folds of the gossamer fabric. Almost like he was looking for something else. His fingers suddenly touched her legs. A shiver of unwilling excitement shimmered through her body. Under the white silk skirt she was still only wearing her thigh-high stockings and a G-string. If he wanted, he could slip his hands up under and touch her. For one crazy second she almost opened her legs to let him.

Good grief, what was *wrong* with her?

Instead, his hands glided down her calves. Slowly. Deliberately. As though he were memorizing every inch of the descent. Her heart pounded. When he reached her ankles he paused, then wrapped his fingers around her crystalline shoes and tugged them off.

With a flick of his wrist they sailed into the narrow space behind the driver's seat. "There. That's better."

She couldn't decide if she felt more outraged, or breathlessly aroused. "Do you manhandle all your clients like this, Mr. Rothchild?"

"Only the ones who need handling," he said with a completely unrepentant smile. He came around and slid behind the wheel. "And it's Conner."

"Not if you're my lawyer, it isn't."

"What, because I'm your attorney we can't be friends?"

She searched his eyes. Which were the exact color of the morning desert, she noticed for the first time. A morning desert in the springtime, when the landscape was at its most beautiful. Falcon brown with flecks of rich green. Surrounded by long, dark lashes, and a sensual tilt to arched brows that matched his movie-star-perfect brown hair.

He was dazzling.

And so colossally out of her universe it made her stomach do crazy somersaults.

His smile widened. "I'll take that as a yes, we can."

Huh?

The engine revved and they took off, were waved through the FBI guard post and drove out onto the street. As they gained speed, the billowing skirt of the wedding dress fluttered up around her shoulders, filling the open convertible.

The night was dark and desert-warm, the winking lights of the Strip just ahead. Rusty mountains ringed the city, sometimes a cozy cocoon that circled the city in its own private haven, sometimes menacing omnipresent watchers of the multitude of sins that went down there in Vegas.

But for now, the bright lights reigned supreme, shiny and colorful, lending the city its famous carnival atmosphere.

As soon as they reached downtown, it started—the honking horns and the shouts and thumbs-up. Tourists waved and whistled. Obviously everyone thought she and Conner were newlyweds, coming straight from some outlandish Las Vegas wedding chapel with a preacher dressed as Elvis or some other zany impersonator.

She wanted to sink right through the soft leather seat and disappear forever. "Damn. I should have changed clothes," she said, chagrined. "Sorry."

Conner waved back to a blue-haired old lady walking with an equally old guy in a pair of screamingly loud plaid shorts. "Don't be. Haven't had this much fun since I drove the UNLV homecoming queen around the football field at halftime."

Figured he did that.

Probably dated her, too.

Probably last year.

Damn.

"How old are you, anyway?" she asked, suddenly irrationally, absurdly and completely inappropriately jealous.

The flashing neon lights of the Strip glinted back at her from his eyes as he smiled. "Thirty-three. You?"

"Twenty-four." Her mouth turned down. "Obviously a little too old for you."

He chuckled. "More like a little too young. I generally prefer my women older, more experienced. Fewer misunderstandings that way."

Red alert, girl. Well. At least he was honest about it. "I'm sure."

"That's a bad thing?"

She sank farther into the seat and scowled. "Not at all. Very considerate of you not to break all those young, impressionable hearts flinging themselves at you. I suspect you could do some genuine damage."

"Hmm. Sounds like you've had yours broken by some insensitive older guy."

The lawyer was too perceptive by half. She shrugged as casually as she could manage. Her heart was none of his damned business.

"I apologize on behalf of all older men," he said. "The jerk must have been a real idiot."

"Which one?" she muttered.

"Ouch." Somehow his hand found hers in the folds of her dress and squeezed it. "Every last one of them."

Their eyes met, and again that weird feeling sifted through her. Part longing, part relief, part visceral hope.

Totally insane.

She pulled her hand away. As seductions went, his technique was pretty low-key. But pretty darn effective. And very dangerous. Already she was wondering what it would feel like to be curled up in his arms, warm and replete after making love to him. To have those amazing feelings of tender belonging she'd gotten just a glimpse of, as they lay skin-to-skin and...

And heaven help her.

He stopped at the red light at Flamingo Road, just up the block from the faux Eiffel Tower. A clutch of tipsy tourists tumbled across the street in front of them. Naturally, the whole group noticed her white dress and started to cheer and clap.

"Kiss the bride!" one of them shouted. Soon they were all whistling and yelling, "Kiss her! Kiss her!"

He turned to grin at her.

Oh. No.

"Don't you dare even *think* ab—"

But his lips were already on hers. Warm. Firm. Tasting of sin and forever. She sucked in a breath of shock as his tongue touched hers, and he took the opening in bold invitation. His hand slid behind her neck and tugged her closer. His other arm banded around her, pulling her upper body tight against him. His tongue invaded her mouth, his fingers held her fast for a deep, lingering kiss the likes of which she'd never, ever experienced.

Oh. No.

The cheers of the onlookers faded as the world around them spun away. Wow. The man could *really* kiss. She was light-headed, dizzy with the taste of him and the feel of his body so close to hers. She couldn't help but want more. She wanted to crawl up into his lap and hold him tight and never let him go.

All too soon his lips lifted and the blaring of car horns and wolf whistles all around invaded her consciousness. She moaned. Unsure if it was the loss of his nearness or the reality of her immense stupidity that made the desperate sound escape her throat.

Oh, what had she done?

And, damn it, now he had that look on his face again. Like she was some kind of apparition or two-headed monster he couldn't quite believe he'd just kissed.

Nope, she sighed, as a slash of hurt ripped her heart once

again. Nothing quite so dramatic. Just an ordinary exotic dancer…make that *stripper*…from the wrong side of the tracks.

Way to go, Mancuso.

He revved the engine, and the car leaped forward. It took about three excruciating minutes to reach her gated apartment complex, where he zoomed into the underground garage and squealed into her parking spot. She was still too flustered and mortified to wonder how he'd known her address—or which slot was hers. He'd only opened his mouth again to confirm that she still lived with Darla. He shut off the engine and the headlights. The dim overhead garage fluorescents flickered and hummed.

She struggled to get the seat belt unfastened but naturally her fingers refused to work. Mentally she scrambled to prepare her Don't-Worry-I've-Already-Forgotten-It-Happened speech when he came around, reached in and unsnapped the belt. Then once again she was swept up in his arms.

"Conner!" she squeaked, clutching her bag of belongings to her chest uncertainly. "I can walk by myself!"

"Not with those ridiculous shoes, you can't. Pure instruments of torture." He looked down at her, an inscrutable look on his face. "Believe it or not, I *am* a gentleman."

His tempting, downturned mouth was dangerously close.

No.

No.

No.

The man had horrified himself by kissing her. Clearly, he didn't want her. She was *so* not going to embarrass herself even further.

He saved her the decision by looking away. And strode through the dark garage toward the lighted elevator without giving her a chance to protest. Her dress billowed. Her heart thundered. He didn't look like he wanted to seduce her. He looked like he wanted to devour her alive. And not in a good way.

The elevator whooshed open, and he carried her into it. He pressed the correct button for her floor—the penthouse, of course. Nothing but the best for Darla.

Darla, who wouldn't be home to run interference for her tonight. Was that why he'd asked?

Oh, great.

She was all on her own. To fend off this overpowering attraction for the most inappropriate man alive. Or…to let him in to break her heart.

She had to get a grip. Fast.

She was just under some weird, arrest-induced erotic spell. This wasn't like her. Not at all. She didn't do flings, or men she'd just met. She didn't even do men she knew well. How could she consider making such a fool of herself over this one who obviously didn't—

"Key," he broke into her chaotic thoughts before they reached the top floor. You couldn't get off at the penthouse without a special key. Naturally, he'd know that.

She juggled her purse out from the bag. Except—

"This isn't my purse. It's Darla's." Her sister must have grabbed the wrong one in her haste to get out of the club.

"Does she have a key?" he asked, his voice deep and dark. Something in his tone sent a shiver tripping down her spine.

She looked up at him. His eyes were smoldering. She faltered and dropped the belongings bag, but managed to hang on to the purse. What was going on here?

"Yes," she stammered, fumbling through its contents. "I—I th-think so."

"Let me have it."

Her pulse jumped a mile. "Conner," she managed, digging out the key and handing it to him. "You're not planning to come in, are you?"

"What do you think?"

He really didn't want to know what she was thinking…

"Please. This is really not a good idea."

"No damn kidding," he shot back. But then his mouth was on hers and she couldn't turn him away if her life depended on it. She moaned in surprise, opening herself to him, and wound her arms around his neck. This was *so* not a good idea. He swung her down so she was sitting on his forearm, and her legs instinctively wrapped around his waist.

The elevator doors opened, and they kissed madly, all the way across the square marble foyer to the penthouse entrance. Her back slammed up against it, and a moment later the door swung open and he followed the solid wood around with her, keeping her back pressed up to it as he devoured her mouth.

The sound of Velcro ripping apart was followed by a whoosh of cool air on her legs and bottom. A billow of white floated to the floor. Another rip and her breakaway top joined it. He groaned, pulling away to look at her spilling out of her lace corset, then his hands found her bare flesh.

They kissed and kissed, and he touched her everywhere. They ground their bodies together in a frenzy of desire. His fingers slid between her legs and parted her blossoming folds. She cried out as he found the center of her need and touched her there.

"That's right, give it to me," he whispered into her mouth. His fingers circled, driving a moan from her. "I want it all."

"Conner," she cried. "Please, I— Nhh…"

It was no use. He was too skilled, too perfect, and she was too aroused to stop the tidal wave of pleasure that crashed over her. She arched, her body shuddering over the edge, and surrendered to the sensation.

He drew it out as long as it would go, playing her flesh like a professional gambler caressed his cards.

By the time he let her slide to her feet, she was trembling

so hard she could hardly see straight. So at first she didn't even notice.

But when he demanded huskily, "Where's your bedroom?" and they turned into the living room, both of them halted dead in their tracks.

The place was in a complete shambles.

"Omigod," she whispered, barely catching her breath.

Someone had broken in. And ransacked the apartment.

On the wall, big sloppy letters had been scrawled in bright red paint.

GIVE IT BACK BITCH OR YOU'LL DIE NEXT.

Chapter 6

Conner took one look at the destruction in front of him and instantly visions of Candace's murder scene slammed through his brain. The wreckage. Her pale face lying in a stain of blood.

Oh, no, please not another victim.

He grabbed Vera and whisked her back out the door and pushed her against the foyer wall.

"Don't move," he admonished as he whipped out his cell phone and Lex Duncan's card from his pocket. "Someone may still be in there." Like Darla. Sprawled dead on the floor as Candace had been. Though he hadn't seen any blood or body in the quick visual scan he'd done. Thank God.

Vera looked like a deer caught in the headlights. "Someone like who?" she asked in a strangled croak, grasping his suit jacket sleeve with both hands.

"Whoever did this," he answered, punching buttons on the phone and trying not to think about what he'd just done with those same fingers. What he'd been *about* to do with them. *Damn.*

"Duncan."

"It's Conner Rothchild. Vera and Darla's place has been broken into," he told the FBI agent. "It looks bad."

Duncan swore. "Darla?"

"Not here that I could see."

"Exit the apartment and wait for me outside," he ordered, then hung up.

"I don't understand," Vera said, her voice cracking. Her eyes filled as he pulled her fully into his arms. "Why would anyone write something that horrible on my wall? Give *what* back?"

"I'm not sure," he said. Though he knew damn well. Silver had received a nearly identical message scrawled on her mirror about being the next one to die—just before someone maliciously brought a scaffolding down on her head. That someone must still be after the Tears of the Quetzal. And didn't know it was now in FBI custody. Until the culprit was found, Vera could be in danger.

Conner gathered her up in his arms again, heading for the elevator. "Let's get you away from here."

For a second she looked like she wanted to object. But then she just put her arms around him and clung to him. Not in a sexual way—despite the fact that she was nearly naked and just moments ago had all but given herself to him—but like a frightened woman would hold a man who made her feel safe.

His stomach roiled into a clot of opposing emotions. Anger at whoever had done this. And a strange, completely alien sense of wanting to protect her from all harm.

Okay, that and a gnawing sense of panic.

Something was going on deep inside him, in his heart, that he did not understand. Did not need. Definitely did not want.

The elevator opened and he swept in, pushed the button for the ground floor.

"Vera," he said. "I know you didn't want me as your lawyer, but I'm hoping you trust me as a friend, after—" He stopped, suddenly feeling awkward. Damn. If not for the break-in, they'd be in bed by now, naked, and he'd be deep inside her. Making love. He was still aroused, still aching for relief. Still wanting her like she was the last woman on earth and he hadn't had sex for at least a decade.

He cleared his throat. "In light of…what happened between us, I'll be turning over your case to my assistant in the morning. Meanwhile, I hope you believe I have your interests as my top priority in this incident."

For once she didn't argue. She bit her lip and nodded. It obviously hadn't occurred to her that her sister might be inside hurt—or worse. He didn't intend to enlighten her. But there were also other issues at hand.

"Here's the thing. The FBI is on its way. Vera, think hard. If there's anything, any reason at all, they shouldn't go into your apartment, you need to tell me now. Before they arrive."

She gazed up at him, her green eyes wide and uncomprehending. Man, she was guileless. Did that mean his instincts were right about her?

"You mean…like drugs or something?" she asked.

Again he cleared his throat, not understanding why it was so damn important to him that she be innocent. "For example, yeah."

She continued to worry her lip. "Um. Darla might not want them in her room. There could be…some illegal substances."

He nodded. No shock there. "They'll probably look the other way on that, this time. Anything else?"

"Like…?"

"Did Duncan tell you any of his suspicions about your sister?" he asked carefully.

"Suspicions of what?"

Okay, apparently not. "I'm not really sure how much I should be revealing to you, but since you're still my client, I feel I should be up-front and warn you. That ring you were wearing isn't the only thing Darla is suspected of stealing. There may be more."

"Stolen jewelry?" she asked, her jaw dropping. "That's not possible. Darla is rich! An heiress. Why would she ever…" Vera's words trickled to a stop.

He gazed down at her. "Could it be true? Because if the FBI finds stolen goods in your apartment, it could get really ugly."

"I don't know," she said worriedly. "Really. I wouldn't have thought so, but…Darla is… Well, sometimes she gets these crazy ideas. For thrills, she says. Or to get back at our father. For his neglect. I suppose…" She looked miserable. "I suppose it could be true. I just don't know. But I don't think anything would be kept here. I would know."

"Fair enough." The elevator doors opened and suddenly he remembered what she was wearing…or rather, *not* wearing. He was about to slip off his jacket to give her when he realized the bag of belongings she'd dropped on the ride up was still lying in the corner of the elevator.

He grabbed it and pressed it into her hands. "Here. Better get dressed before someone sees you."

"Oh, jeez," she said, glancing down at herself. "Not exactly street attire."

More's the pity. He admired how she was so totally comfortable in her own bare skin. The women he knew would be dying of embarrassment to be seen like this in public, every last one, convinced their bodies were too fat or too skinny or had some other terrible imagined flaw, making them unduly self-conscious. Women could have such hang-ups about their self-image. It was refreshing to be around one who so obviously liked how she looked.

She quickly pulled on the jeans and T-shirt. He forced himself to concentrate. "You stay down here in the lobby and wait for Duncan. I'll go back to the apartment and take a quick look around. If there's anything that shouldn't be found, I'll deny him permission to search there. Okay?"

Fear leaped into her eyes. "You're leaving me alone? Why can't I go with you?"

"Just in case," he said, and she looked even more panicked. "Don't worry, you'll be fine. Duncan will get here in a few minutes." Unable to help himself, he bent down and kissed her. The taste of her lips swirled on his tongue, and a painful ache of arousal swept through him again. *Too good.* He pulled away.

"Conner, wait," she began. She glanced down at his mouth, and then his body, and something shifted in her expression. Uh-oh, trouble ahead. "I, um, don't—"

He put a finger to her lips. "Shh. We'll talk later, all right? I've got to go up."

She nodded reluctantly. "What if someone's up there with a gun?" she asked nervously.

"Anyone's probably long gone," he assured her, then led her out of the elevator, gave her a last kiss and got back on.

Watching him unhappily, she wrapped her arms around her middle. "Please, be careful."

He smiled, touched by the sincere worry in her eyes. "Count on it."

Once up in the apartment, he was able to give the whole penthouse a cursory search before the FBI showed up. No Darla, thank heaven. Nothing else out of the ordinary was visible in the piles of debris left by the break-in or in any of the bedrooms, either, so granting Duncan and his CSI techs access would not compromise his client.

He took one last look around. If the place hadn't been such a mess, it would have been really nice. If nothing else, Darla had good taste. At least in interior decorating. In friends and lifestyle, maybe not so much.

Of course, an exotic dancer would normally be included in his general condemnation. In the Las Vegas legal community, aside from his take-no-prisoners ruthlessness in the courtroom, Conner was known for a generous pro bono policy toward the homeless, drug addicts and sex workers. But he'd never considered them his equals in any sense of the word. His family would disown him if they even suspected he was considering a serious liaison with a stripper…even if she was the illegitimate daughter of billionaire Maximillian St. Giles.

Hell, *especially* if she was the illegitimate daughter of Maximillian St. Giles. Or any other woman not in his social class or better. The key word there was *illegitimate*. His father had given Uncle Harold a lifetime of grief for marrying beneath him. More than once. Conner had no intention of repeating that mistake and lowering his father's respect for him. Or giving his blue-blood family any reason to question Conner's loyalty to their highbrow ideals, even if he thought they were at times silly and sometimes destructive.

He'd seen firsthand what those kind of elitist notions could do to families. Look at Candace. He was convinced she'd still be alive today if she hadn't been summarily dismissed from the family fold after marrying Jack Cortland, the druggie rock-star boy. Those two poor kids of hers. God only knew what would become of them without the support of family, with only a questionable father to raise them, stuck out on some ranch in the middle of nowhere.

Anyway. Under all the broken glassware and china, disheveled books and shelf items and knife-slit, unstuffed cushions and furniture, Conner recognized a beautiful living space, subtly sophisticated and timelessly chic. He didn't know why that surprised him, but it did. Pleasantly so. *Some* of Darla's wealthy upbringing must have rubbed off on her, after all.

He gave a wry sigh. That probably explained why she'd gone after the Tears of the Quetzal. The ring was the classiest piece of jewelry he'd ever laid eyes on. And now it had passed from Vera's finger straight into FBI custody. Forget about retrieving it any time soon. *That* place was like Fort Knox. Uncle Harold was not going to be pleased.

The sound of the elevator approaching pulled Conner back to the situation at hand. He went out to the foyer and met Special Agent Duncan as he exited the lift, followed by two other men in white jumpsuits carrying CSI cases. Vera popped out like a nervous jack-in-the-box.

"Are you okay?" she asked him before Duncan could open his mouth. "Did you see anyone? Any more messages written on the walls? Talk to me!"

"Whoa, slow down," he admonished gently and put an arm around her shoulder. "No more graffiti. No sign of the intruders," he told Duncan, and gave a surreptitious shake of his head at the agent's silent query about Darla.

Duncan looked relieved, then gave Conner's protective arm a brief, disapproving frown.

"Not that it's any of your business," Conner said to stave off any comments, "but I'm turning over Vera's case to an associate so there's no conflict of interest."

Duncan's frown deepened as he signaled the CSI techs to proceed into the penthouse to get started. "That wasn't part of our deal," he said.

"What deal?" Vera asked.

"Nothing's changed," Conner assured him. "Can we just—"

"What deal?" Vera asked again, more insistently. She turned under his arm to look up at him.

"Never mind—"

Duncan addressed her. "For your release."

"What about it?" she asked, eyes narrowing.

Damn. *So* not good.

"Rothchild agreed to help us bring Darla St. Giles into custody. He promised to call us when she contacts you."

Ah, hell.

Shock went through her expression. She stepped away from him angrily. "Oh, really. What makes you think she'll contact me? And even if she does, what makes you think I'll tell you? How dare you! What would make you agree to such a thing?" Her voice was getting louder and louder.

"Vera, please believe me, it was for your own good."

"My own *good?*" she spat out. "Are you *kidding* me? Betraying my sister?"

"He's right," Duncan interjected stonily. "You were apprehended with the Rothchild's diamond on your finger. Until it can be established exactly how it got there, *you* are our—"

"Wait just a cotton-picking minute!" Her expression went even more furious. She glared at Conner. "The *Rothchild's* diamond? That was *your* ring?"

He was in *such* deep trouble. "My family's, yes. But—"

She looked like he had slapped her across the face. Hard. "And you were going to tell me this little detail *when?*"

"Vera, who the ring belongs to is not what's important here."

"My God, Conner! If *that's* not a conflict of interest, I don't know what is! And you expect me to trust you? What else are you lying to me about?"

It was his turn to be indignant. "That's not fair. I never lied to you."

"I may not be some rich, fancy-schmancy lawyer, but even I know what lying by omission means," she ground out. "And to think I—" Her mouth snapped shut, and she squeezed her eyes closed.

He fisted his hands on his hips, ignoring the all-too-personal dig. "Do you recall in the club when I said I had information about your sister? I was going to tell you then, but was interrupted when…let's see…oh, yeah, you got *arrested!*"

"Speaking of which." Duncan stepped between them. "Why exactly were you at the Diamond Lounge in the first place, Rothchild? Quite a coincidence, wouldn't you say?" The FBI agent's tone was neutral, but his meaning was unmistakable.

Conner tamped down on his quickly rising hackles. Forced himself into composed, professional lawyer mode. "Are you by any chance asking me for an alibi?" he asked coolly. "For this?" He swept a hand toward the mess in the apartment.

Duncan lifted a shoulder. "It occurs to me that a Rothchild would have the strongest motive to search Miss St. Giles's home. Missing family heirloom, and all. And you being convinced she stole it." He looked smug. "It would also explain your presence at the Diamond Lounge. You didn't find the ring when you searched the apartment and Darla had disappeared, so you took a chance her sister might know where she went."

Damn. It all sounded *far* too plausible.

Except it was all bull, and Duncan knew it. They both knew whoever did this was the same person who'd stalked and almost killed Silver. And possibly Candace. But, okay, he played along.

"Just one thing wrong with your theory," Conner said evenly. "I had no idea Darla had a sister. Oh, and the fact that I *do* have an alibi. I was working another case. The Parker case, if you want to call my firm. I spent the whole afternoon asking questions of the dancers up and down the Strip. At least a couple hundred witnesses, plus video surveillance, I'm sure. The Diamond Lounge was my next stop." He held up a hand. "And, yes, I do have a checked-off list to prove it. Thank you. Thank you very much."

At least Duncan cracked a smile. Vera was still glaring at Conner.

"Okay," Duncan said. "I'll get that checked out, but I believe you're telling the truth. Meanwhile, I still have the problem of Ms. Mancuso. Because if *you* didn't do the break-in…"

Conner nodded. "It was most likely the same guy who's been after the ring since it disappeared from Candace's hand the night she died."

Duncan nodded, too. "A thief whom Darla seems to have double-crossed. And since the FBI now has the ring in its custody—"

"He didn't find it in his search. And since Darla has disappeared—"

"He'll be looking for Ms. Mancuso next, thinking she knows where to find her sister, and therefore the ring."

Vera had been watching the back-and-forth like a spectator at a tennis match, but now she finally caught on with a gasp. "Are you saying…I could be in danger?"

"Did you *read* the message he left on the wall?" Conner queried.

"This man has already gone on the attack for the ring," Duncan said. "Don't take any chances with your safety."

"So what am I supposed to do?"

"Ms. Mancuso was released into your recognizance, Rothchild." Duncan turned to remind him. "And the terms of her bail still stand. But if you prefer, I'll take her back into custody. I can't risk losing my only suspect. In any manner."

"What? Hold on!" Vera exclaimed. "His recognizance or police custody? There has to be a door number three here."

"I respect your dilemma, Ms. Mancuso," the agent said. "But the only reason you are not in a cell right now is because of Mr. Rothchild's spotless reputation as an attorney and his formidable social standing in the community. I've already stretched the law as far as I'm willing to go in that regard. He stays with you or you come with me."

There was a pregnant pause, the silence in the marble foyer only broken by the sounds of the CSI techs' cameras clicking inside the apartment.

"Fine," she said at length, but obviously mad as a hornet. "I'll move a futon for him out into the vestibule." She rounded on Conner. "You can set it up in front of the elevator so there's no way I—or anyone else—can slip past—"

His brows shot up. *Excuse me?* He shoved aside the insult. "You *want* to stay in a ransacked apartment?"

"Like I have a choice?" she fired back.

"Sorry," Duncan interrupted. "Not possible. No one's allowed into the apartment until the techs are finished processing for trace and fingerprints. That'll take at least a few hours."

"She'll stay at my place," Conner said through clamped teeth, ready to strangle the woman. A freakin' futon? He didn't *think* so.

She opened her mouth to protest but he nipped it. "I have plenty of room. And can provide an armed guard," he added pointedly.

"Good," Duncan said, passing Conner his notebook. "Write down the address and phone number."

Almost sputtering, she crossed her arms over her ample chest. Sending an untimely reminder through his body that he was still more than half-aroused. But her vehement, "I am *not* going anywhere with you," jerked him right out of his momentary hormonal stupor.

Which probably made him point out more sharply than

strictly necessary, "I happen to know you have no money and nowhere else to go." He ignored her gasp and went on, "And if you think I'm paying for a hotel when I have ten bedrooms sitting empty at my house, you're dead wrong."

She blinked and her eyes shuttered. He realized too late he'd reacted like a defense attorney, trampling her objections like a charging rhino. And he'd hurt her.

Well, too damn bad. She'd hurt him first.

He pushed out a calming breath, chagrined at his childish outburst.

God.

Was he actually whining like a two-year-old?

"I'm sorry," he said gruffly. "That was a thoughtless and unnecessary remark. But the reality is, it's my house or jail."

She looked like a Nile cat chased into a tree by that charging rhino. Angry. Cornered. But undefeated. "In that case," she said with chin held high, "I'll take jail."

Chapter 7

Vera stared up at the stunning mansion in front of her.

Holy mackerel.

The rising sun was just peeking over the desert horizon, spreading a magical spill of golden light over the soft coral-colored adobe walls and arches of the Southwest-inspired manor house and surrounding lush green lawns and gardens.

"You live here?" she asked her jailer. *"Alone?"*

They were the first words she'd spoken to Conner Biggest-Bully-in-the-Universe Rothchild since she'd grudgingly hunched into the passenger seat of his ridiculously ostentatious car to be driven here. To his house. Where he lived.

How she'd let herself get talked into going *anywhere* with the lying jerk, let alone his own home, she'd never know.

Okay, not true. It was the work of the usual catch-22: absence of money, family or personal influence.

Story of her life.

"Alone, yes. But I have a lot of friends who visit," he answered her rhetorical question.

She just bet he did.

Never mind that ninety-eight percent of the women in the state of Nevada would kill to take her place. Or that *Las Vegas Magazine*'s official Most Eligible Bachelor was undoubtedly the sexiest, most attractive man breathing on this earth. Vera knew very well when she was outclassed, outplayed and miles out of her comfort zone. About ten-and-a-half miles to be exact—the distance between the mobile home park where she'd grown up and Conner Rothchild's sprawling, multimillion-dollar neighborhood.

No, Vera Mancuso had no freaking business being in this place, with this man.

"Must be nice," she responded as he drove through the ten-foot-tall iron security gate, which closed automatically behind the car. "And you have a lot of family, too, from what I hear. Quite the Las Vegas dynasty, the Rothchilds."

"Don't believe everything you read in the tabloids," he said, pulling to a stop under the entry's porte cochere.

"I don't," she assured him. "My information comes straight from the horse's mouth."

"Oh?" He gave her a mildly curious hike of an eyebrow as he opened the car door for her and helped her out.

"Darla was good friends with your cousins Candace and Silver. I still have lunch with Silver occasionally."

"Ah."

She stopped suddenly and turned back to his car. Before leaving the apartment, the CSI techs had packed her a small overnight bag, including a pair of flip-flops, but she needed her stage shoes for work tonight. They were still behind the seat where he'd tossed them back at FBI headquarters. "I'd like my shoes back, please. From last night."

"Of course." He leaned over the side of the car to fish them out.

Oh, boy.

His suit pants stretched over his tight backside, revealing every luscious dip and muscle of that tasty bit of anatomy. She had to stuff her hands under her armpits to keep from touching.

He handed her the glasslike shoes with a wry smile. "Don't lose one, Cinderella," he teased.

She made a face and snatched them from his hand. "You know, she talked about you all the time. Your cousin Candace."

"Did she, now." He took her overnight bag and led her up the mansion's sweeping front steps.

"She didn't like you very much."

"Now there's a shock." He did something with his key chain, and the ornately carved entry door swung open.

"She said you're mean, stubborn and ruthless and will do anything to get your clients off."

"Never a good thing in a lawyer," he said dryly. "After you."

She met his amused gaze, so strong and confident. Not to mention devoid of shadiness or deceit. With a sinking feeling she suddenly knew Candace was completely wrong about him.

She shouldn't be surprised. The rivalry between the Rothchild family cousins was legendary in Vegas, where each sought to outdo the other in glamour, media notoriety and wild living. Conner was no exception. He regularly figured in the gossip columns.

But Vera, of all people, was acutely aware that a public image did not always reflect the real person. Although she got along with Candace okay, and Darla adored her, Candace always did have a family ax to grind.

"Touché," Vera acknowledged, thinking just maybe *she'd* been wrong about Conner, too.

Not good. She did *not* want to like this man. Bad enough

she was so hopelessly attracted to him physically. How depressing would it be to have him turn out to be honorable and principled, too?

He ushered her in. "Welcome to my home."

Said the spider to the fly.

"Wow," she murmured, stepping into a stunning showplace of glossy, contemporary elegance. Clutching her shoes in her hand, she walked from the soaring foyer into a grand salon and did a slow three-sixty, totally awestruck. She'd decorated Darla's penthouse because when she'd moved in it had white walls and hotel furniture, and she'd been darn proud of the results. But this…this was utterly gorgeous. "Nice place," she managed.

He chuckled. "Apparently I live for nice."

Just then, an older woman in a fuzzy robe hurried into the room. "Oh, Mr. Conner, sir! I didn't expect you back tonight."

"Sorry to wake you so early, Hildy," he said in warm apology. "This is Vera. She'll be spending a few days with me."

Days?

"Certainly, sir."

The housekeeper didn't even bat an eyelash. Obviously not unusual for her employer to bring home women at the crack of dawn and announce they'd be spending more than one night chez Conner. Vera ground her teeth. Well, what did she expect?

"Will you be needing anything, sir? Coffee, or…?" Hildy asked.

"No, nothing, thanks. Just sleep." He handed her Vera's overnight bag, and the woman turned to go.

"Uh," Vera interjected before it was too late, "by 'with me' what Mr. Rothchild really meant was 'here.' As in 'here,' but in a separate bedroom. And 'here,' but as far away as possible from where he sleeps." She pasted on a smile.

This time Hildy did blink. And glanced at Conner for confirmation.

His mouth quirked. "As the lady says. You can put her in the guest cabana. That should be far enough away."

Hildy's eyes met hers for a split second, and Vera could have sworn the older lady was holding back a smirk. Vera wondered idly if she'd just joined the ranks of Too-Stupid-To-Live, or Girl Folk Hero....

"Oh, well. I need the sleep anyway," he said philosophically when the housekeeper had gone. "You'll like the cabana. It's very private out there. But don't get any bright ideas about escaping. I was serious about the armed guard. I've already called the security company."

She didn't know whether to be insulted or flattered. "Don't worry. I took Agent Duncan's warning to heart."

Before leaving the penthouse, the FBI man had cautioned her against going anywhere alone, or without Conner's permission, for her own safety. After finding out about the connection between the stolen ring and the murder of Candace Rothchild and attack on Silver Rothchild, the whole 'Give it back or you'll die next bitch' thing was plenty to convince Vera not to take any chances.

"I don't know why you didn't just let Duncan put me in jail," she said without thinking.

Then she remembered.

Whoops. Yeah, she did know. Because Conner'd expected to have sex with her, that's why. Which would surely have happened had it not been for the timely interruption of the break-in and the subsequent revelations into his motives for seeking her out in the first place.

She'd so totally lost her mind in that elevator. Thank God she'd found it since.

More or less.

Though being reminded of the delicious things he'd done to her during her temporary insanity wasn't helping.

She looked up and realized he was gazing at her sardonically, his thoughts as transparent as hers apparently were.

"Forget it." She wagged a finger. "No bodyguard necessary. Literally or otherwise. I saw the size of the fence around this place, and the only person I'm in danger from here is you." And possibly herself.

"Only thinking of your safety," he said amenably.

"Sure you are."

Seeking a distraction, she glanced around the glamorous room, filled with the trappings of wealth, and was suddenly struck with a pang of regret. What would it be like to be part of this world, even for a few days...or nights? Would it be such a sacrifice to sleep with him, to find out?

God, no. Not in the least. The man was to die for. And she'd be using him just as much as he was using her. But...

"I'm sorry, casual sex isn't something I do." She felt the need to explain, but it came with a belated inward wince. "Embarrassing evidence to the contrary."

He smiled. "Nothing embarrassing about it. In fact, it was pretty damn hot if you ask me. For, you know, not being casual sex."

She actually felt a flush work its way up her throat to her cheeks. Good grief. When was the last time she'd blushed?

Help.

"You said something about a guest house? I really should get some sleep or I'll be a mess at work tonight." She sighed. "Assuming I still have a job."

He looked surprised. "You're going back there?"

"Hell, yeah. If the boss will let me. I have no choice, Conner. I have bills to pay. Money doesn't grow on trees." She glanced around again. "Well, for some of us anyway."

He ignored the barb and rubbed a hand over his mouth. "Okay. I guess I can do that."

"You? What do you mean?"

"So quickly they forget."

"Oh. Right." They were stuck like glue until Special Agent Duncan decided to arrest her. Which meant Conner'd have to come to the club with her.

A memory washed over her, of him sitting in the front row sipping champagne like a dissolute sultan, watching her take off every stitch of clothing. And—oh, God—how turned on she'd been. By him. By his negligent air of wealth and power. And the hungry look in his eyes as his gaze had caressed her nude body. No wonder she'd gone off like a rocket when he touched her later on.

She swallowed. "I suppose you'll insist on going with me."

"Oh, absolutely. Wouldn't miss it." He winked.

That's what she was afraid of.

That, and the nutcase who might now be after her because of that damn ring. Maybe it wasn't such a bad idea he went with her, after all.

Bad enough she'd invaded his dreams all night like some kind of teasing succubus, but even now, the next morning, sun shining, birds singing, the little witch was still torturing him. Deliberately. With malice aforethought.

Conner frowned, taking in the sight that had nearly made the tray of coffee and croissants he was carrying spill all over the Mexican patio tiles. The French doors to the cabana had been flung open. Sheer curtains billowed out from them in the hot desert breeze. Inside the dim room, the scene was straight out of one of the erotic dreams he'd been haunted by all night.

Vera. Nude. Sprawled on her stomach across her bed… Except in his dreams of course it had been *his* bed. Sheets in a tangle. Her skin moist with a sheen of sweat. Her hair in a mess as though from his fingers… Except his fingers had unfortunately been nowhere near her last night.

Seeing her like that, he'd been shocked enough that his first thought was that she was dead. Lying there brutally murdered, like his cousin Candace. The memory of that crime scene had streaked through his mind, nearly tipping the tray in his hands. Thankfully she'd stirred immediately at the sound of the rattling dishes so he knew she was okay, or he would really have lost it.

As it was, he was now close to losing it for an entirely different reason.

The woman was a sensual vision. Her hot body even sexier than in his dreams.

Easy, boy.

She'd made it clear last night she was no longer interested in sex with him. He'd honored her wishes and hadn't pushed it, although he was pretty sure he could have changed her mind with very little effort. They obviously had chemistry. Potent chemistry. And lots of it.

But this…this was unfair.

Or maybe it was an invitation? Had she gone to bed naked, hoping he would come to her?

What an idiot. He should at least have tried…

"Conner?"

He started at the sound of her throaty, sleep-muzzy voice. The dishes rattled, and he had to catch the tray for the second time to keep from dumping it.

"Yeah. It's me."

She turned over in the bed, and he gripped the tray even harder. *Pure torture.* "What have you got?"

Besides a hard-on? "Breakfast," he croaked. "Interested?"

"Mmm." Her arms rose in a languorous stretch. "Coffee, I hope?"

Lord, help him.

"Yep." He reached a nearby patio table just in time, depositing the tray on the round glass top with a clatter. After righting the cups and returning the croissants to the plate, he turned, ready to abandon all pretense and just go in and devour her, when she strolled by with another stretch, heading for the pool.

"I feel divine! Haven't slept so well in ages," she declared, pushing her mane of chestnut hair back from her face. "I love sleeping with the doors open, with the warm air and the smell of the desert. Haven't been able to do that since I sold the mobile home."

He paused, nonplussed. Okay. Obviously *not* an invitation. He grappled for a thread of conversation that didn't involve the words *condom* or *go down*. "Mobile home?" he asked.

She shot him a look, stopping at the edge of the pool and dipping a toe into it. A toe that was bare, just like the rest of her. "I grew up in the Sunnyvale Mobile Home Park, just outside of town."

He knew that. He was just momentarily brain-dead. "No air-conditioning?" he ventured.

She smiled. "No."

She executed a perfect dive into the water. He let out a long, long breath, and for a few minutes he watched her expertly cut through the water, the joy in her movements contagious. He wanted to join her in the worst way, but in a sense it would have been like some fool painting daisies into a Monet. Perfection spoiled. He forced himself onto a patio chair, peeled off his shirt because he was suddenly far too warm and poured coffee instead.

She bobbed up at the side of the pool, folding her arms along the coping. "Hope you don't mind. I couldn't resist a quick dip. We have a pool in our apartment building, but it's indoors." She wrinkled her nose as though that were a cardinal sin.

"Take all the time you like. I'm enjoying the view."

She tilted her head. "Not misinterpreting, I hope."

"I'll have to admit," he said, taking a sip of strong black coffee to jolt his mind back up where it belonged, "your…lack of inhibition did take me in a certain direction. I now stand corrected."

She smiled and lithely hoisted herself from the water and onto the deck in one fluid movement. Like Venus rising from the sea. She padded to the table with water flowing from her lightly tanned skin like drops of molten gold, and reached for his cup. She put it to her lips with eyes closed and long lashes sparkling with water droplets. He had to grip the arms of his chair to keep from surging to his feet to lick them off. Along with the rivulets trickling down her perfect breasts.

He stifled a groan.

She set the cup down on the table. "Give me a minute," she said. "I'll get dressed." Then she disappeared into the cabana.

He cleared his throat, found his voice and called after her, "Don't bother on my account!"

And he knew then if he hadn't before—which deep down he had, but up until this very moment had chosen total, blind denial. One thing was for damned certain.

He had to have her.

Really *have* her. All to himself. For a few days. A week. Maybe even a month. Long enough to explore that chatter-box mouth with its guileless smile, that amazingly sensual body and the wonderfully sassy woman inside it.

Oh, yeah. He'd have her, all right.

He'd find a way to make her want him.

And the sooner the better.

Or he might just go completely out of his mind.

Chapter 8

"I have a proposition for you."

Vera halted her coffee cup halfway to her mouth and glanced at Conner. "What kind of proposition?" she asked. Like she couldn't guess.

Frankly, she'd been expecting this. She was actually surprised he'd managed to hold out as long as he had. Nearly a whole hour. While they'd talked of her childhood, his crazy relationship with his famous cousins and what it was like to stare up at the night sky out in the vast desert and see a billion gazillion stars up there and wonder if there was any other life in the universe.

Nevertheless, disappointment sifted through her. For some unfathomable reason, she'd thought he might be different from all the other men who tried to get in her pants. She'd *hoped* he was different. He'd been lost in thought for the past few minutes, and she'd really believed he was adjusting his perception of her. Starting to see her as a whole person and not just a nude body onstage or an easy seduction in an elevator.

Oh, well.

"More like an exchange of services," he explained.

"Uh-huh."

Her expression must have betrayed her skepticism, because he rushed to say, "I'd pay you, of course."

She set down her cup very, very carefully. "For what, Conner?"

He exhaled. "You know that deal I made with Duncan for your release? Well, there was more to it than just reporting in on Darla's movements."

Okay, he'd managed to surprise her. Not that this sounded much better than some kind of sexual favor. "Like what?" she asked cautiously.

"I promised I'd help him find out about the jewel theft ring Darla's allegedly part of. Try to narrow down suspects for him."

"I told you I don't know anything about that."

"But I'd like your help investigating."

"Me?"

"I've been thinking about how much you look like Darla. It's obvious you're her sister. You could get people to talk to you. A lot easier than I could."

"But I don't know anyone involved," she said. "Who would I talk to?"

"That's what I need your help figuring out. I'll bet someone from her circle of friends is either in on the jewelry thefts or knows something about the ring of thieves doing them. You've met most of her friends, right?"

"Well. Not really. Only the ones who've been to parties at our apartment or who we've occasionally gone out with together, like to casinos or clubs. But that doesn't happen very often. And very few know I'm her sister. We've mostly passed off our resemblance just as a fun coincidence."

He tilted his head. "Really? And she didn't invite you to other people's parties? Social events? That sort of thing?"

She glanced away. To her credit, Darla *had* invited her to lots of things. Vera had even gone. Once. And stood in a corner the whole time paralyzed with feelings of inadequacy. "I don't really fit into her social stratosphere."

He regarded her for a moment. "Her evaluation or yours?"

"Mine," she admitted with a shrug. "And my father's. He threatened to disown Darla if she spread it around that he'd spawned an illegitimate child. He'd make my life hell if it got out."

"I assume you're talking about Maximillian St. Giles."

"Daddy dearest." She sighed. After twenty-four years, you'd think she'd be used to the hurt. But it still cut like a shard of glass to the heart when she thought about his categorical rejection.

"What could he possibly have against you?" Conner asked, echoing the question she'd asked herself a thousand times. Always with the same answer.

She looked back at Conner. "I take my clothes off for a living. And I suppose I remind him of his vulnerability. Or failings. Or both."

"And whose fault is all that? Not yours." He shook his head. "The man's a dolt. If I had a daughter as smart, gorgeous and determined as you, I'd be showing her off to everyone, not hiding her away like she was something to be ashamed of. I wouldn't care how she came into the world."

Vera blinked, blindsided by the sincere indignation in Conner's voice…on her behalf. No one had ever defended her honor so vehemently. No one.

She swallowed the lump that welled up in her throat. "Thanks. Too bad he's not quite as broad-minded as you are."

"That settles it," Conner said, folding his arms over his chest and surveying her with a resolute smile. "No argument. You're coming with me."

Alarm zinged up her spine. "Where?"

"The Lights of Las Vegas Charity Ball on Friday night."

He had to be kidding. The Lights of Las Vegas Charity Ball was the biggest annual charity fund-raiser in the city; everyone who was anyone went—provided you were a gazillionaire or a famous star of some sort.

"What, *me?* No! *Hell,* no. Are you nuts?"

"All of Darla's friends will be there. It's the perfect opportunity for you to ask questions. Hey!" he exclaimed with growing excitement. "Maybe the thieves are planning to work the event and we can catch them in the act."

"One small problem."

"What's that?"

"Aside from the fact that I'd never in a million years be able to pull it off, I work Friday. It's our biggest night."

He waved a hand in the air dismissively. "I'll pay you better. Name your fee."

"*And* I have nothing to wear that doesn't fasten with Velcro," she added wryly.

"With a clothes allowance."

God, so tempting. He waggled his eyebrows, and for a nanosecond she actually considered it. Then she shook her head. "I can't. Honestly. I'd be lost at one of those fancy society bashes. I wouldn't have the faintest idea what to do or how to conduct myself. People would laugh—"

He took her hand in his over the table and gazed intently at her. "Trust me, no one will laugh. Not after I'm done with you."

Her eyes widened. "What do you mean?"

"Ever see *My Fair Lady?*"

She gave him a withering smile and yanked back her hand.

"Yeah, and look what happened to Eliza Doolittle at the horse race. I rest my case."

He chuckled. "The difference being, you wouldn't need to change a single thing. Just be yourself as you ask around after Darla. Say she's disappeared and as her roommate, you're worried about her."

"I wouldn't be lying. I *am* worried."

"Good. Then you'll do it."

She pushed out a breath, still unconvinced. "What if my father shows up?"

"You leave Maximillian St. Giles to me. C'mon, Vera. Take a chance. Be Cinderella for a night. Hell, you've even got the perfect shoes."

She laughed at his handsome, open face and charmingly amused smile. And felt herself weaken.

She shouldn't.

God knew, she had no business even pretending to belong at a highbrow event like that. Let alone with a man like Conner Rothchild.

"You're wrong about Darla," she said. "If I go to that ball, it's only for one reason. To prove my sister isn't a criminal."

"Fair enough," he said. "It's a deal." He looked at her triumphantly. "So, when can we go shopping?"

Silk. Satin. Lace. Bamboo, for crying out loud. When had they started making clothes out of bamboo, anyway?

Vera had never felt so uncomfortable in her life. Not even the first time she'd gone onstage at that seedy titty bar five years ago and taken off every stitch in front of a pack of drooling men had she felt this vulnerable. At least onstage *she* was in control.

"Utterly stunning," the duchesslike boutique owner said with a satisfied smile at her creation. Meaning the slinky, floor-length evening gown clinging to Vera's every curve. "What do you think, Mr. Rothchild?"

He considered. "I think the neckline could be lower."

"No way," Vera muttered. "Any lower and you'd have to call it a waistline."

"So charming," the duchess cooed. "Your lady friend's modesty becomes her, my dear."

Get me out of here.

"Yes," he deadpanned. "It's one of my favorite things about her."

"I'm standing right here, you know," she said evenly, shooting him a warning glare.

"Well, which gown do you like best? The blue, the red, the gold or the white?" he asked with an unrepentant smile, motioning with a twirled finger for her to spin around one more time in the blue one she was wearing. She grudgingly obliged.

She'd tried on about a thousand different dresses over the past three hours at a dozen or more trendy boutiques before finding a designer Conner approved of, and he had narrowed it down to four choices. Vera hadn't dared voice an opinion other than about the ones she didn't care for, because she had no clue what was expected at the Lights of Las Vegas Charity Ball. Each event on the Vegas social calendar had its own dress code, known only to the city's Chosen Ones. If you violated the Code, people knew and smirked at you behind your back. Or so she'd surmised from the stories of fashion faux pas Darla had come home telling with a superior air of glee.

"They're all exquisite," Vera said. And meant it. "And all far too expensive." And meant that, too. The dresses in this store were so expensive they didn't even have price tags. "You should donate the money to the charity instead."

He signaled the boutique owner to give them a minute alone, then smiled at Vera indulgently. "I've already made out the check, and trust me, this wouldn't even put a dent in it. Besides, I want my assistant to be the most stunning woman there."

Assistant? Oka-ay.

"You wouldn't deny me that satisfaction, would you?" he asked.

She ignored the deliberate hint his slight emphasis on the word *that* carried. "So I take it this isn't a date," she casually said.

"Definitely not. I'm paying you," he said oh-so-reasonably. "I wouldn't want there to be any…misinterpretations."

Ha-ha. The man was hilarious. And transparent as glass.

"Good," she said with a quick smile, not falling for the ploy. "Keeping it business is for the best." Though that did make her stomach sink a little with disappointment. "And since this is on your dime, boss, *you* choose which gown you like best."

"Very well. If you insist."

He studied her again from head to toe, taking so long she was in danger of melting under his scrutiny. The man had a way of undressing her with those dreamy bedroom eyes that made her toes curl and her mouth go dry. Which was a pretty good trick, considering her profession.

"You are so incredibly beautiful," he said at last and looked up with a funny little smile.

Surprise washed through her at the heartfelt compliment. "Thank you," she said, flustered by the admiration lingering in his eyes as he continued to gaze at her. "For everything." She went up on her tiptoes and gave him a soft kiss on the mouth. "You're being so generous, I don't know what to say."

He smiled and kissed her back—a gentle, easy kiss. Then pushed a lock of hair behind her ear. "You've said it. Thank you is plenty."

"I really do feel like Cinderella getting ready for the ball."

His smile went roguish. He brushed his knuckles down her

bare arms, producing a shower of goose bumps. "So, if you're Cinderella, who does that make me?"

He was so fishing. "My fairy godmother?" she suggested impishly.

He made a face. "Not exactly what I was going for."

She grinned, her heart spinning in her chest. "I don't recall reading anywhere that Cinderella was Prince Charming's *assistant.*"

"And I don't remember her being such a smart-aleck." He tapped her on the end of the nose. "Get changed and I'll settle up."

"Aren't you going to tell me which dress you chose?"

"Nope. It'll be a surprise."

"No fair."

He winked. "Who said anything about fair?" Then he was gone from the dressing room.

She eased out a long breath to slow her fluttering heart. Who, indeed? Nothing was fair about this whole situation. Not Darla involving her in felony theft. Not having to go to this stupid ball and make a fool of herself. Certainly not the fact that she was falling hard and fast for Conner Rothchild, a man so breathtakingly wrong for her it defied all odds. Talk about a fairy tale! Too bad Cinderella was just a story. The kind that *didn't* happen in real life.

She really had to make herself remember that. Because after Conner was finished with her, no longer needed her help to fulfill his obligations to the FBI, she knew darn well the magical bubble she'd been floating in would morph back into a pumpkin. It would leave her standing alone, right back where she'd always been. And the only glass slippers she'd be trying on would be on a stage along with a fake wedding dress.

But in the meantime, she had no choice. She must go

through with this. Darla would be the one to suffer if she wimped out and didn't help prove her sister's innocence.

No, she was well and truly stuck in this crazy situation. So she may as well try to enjoy the ride as best she could. Prince Charming and all.

She just hoped she could hang on to her heart—and not let Conner Rothchild steal it along the way.

Chapter 9

Traffic was a bitch. Parking was even worse.

"Just drop me off," Vera told Conner after glancing at the dashboard clock for the tenth time in as many minutes.

He knew she was worried about being late for her shift, convinced her boss was looking for an excuse to fire her after she'd been hauled off by the FBI yesterday. To tell the truth, Conner wished she *would* get fired. She was better than that job. Did not belong at the Diamond Lounge—or anywhere else she had to bare her breasts to make a decent living.

Oh, she'd told him all about her lack of education and her stepfather's Alzheimer's and thus the need to keep him in an assisted-living facility. Conner understood her reasons. He did. He was just unconvinced she had no other recourse. She'd simply had no one tell her about other options.

He planned to. As soon as they'd put this FBI mess behind them, he'd show her how she didn't have to continue in the same vicious cycle as her mother'd been stuck in. There were ways out. To that end, this afternoon he'd paid the bill for the retirement home for the next month. Call it a bonus for her help. That would give her a few weeks' breathing room to help him. It was the least he could do.

Actually…it was far more than he *should* be doing. More than he'd ever done for a client before. He'd always prided himself on staying aloof from the all-too-unfair predicaments life had heaped upon many of his clients…hell, most of his clients. He was a defense attorney. People who did crimes had myriad reasons for committing them, but none of those reasons were fair or happy. Like a doctor with his patients, a good attorney needed to distance himself from the world of hurt he dealt with every day. Treat everyone as a case number, even as he helped them.

But Vera was different. She affected him like no one ever had. As a representative of the law—and as a man. She was incredibly smart, grounded and determined. Not to mention the hottest woman he'd ever met.

He was in deep trouble here.

"Seriously," she said, "I can walk to the club. It's just a couple of blocks. It'll be faster than this mess."

No doubt correct. Sundown on the Strip was a giant traffic jam. "All right," he said, though he didn't like the notion of her being on her own for even a minute. Whoever was stalking the Tears of the Quetzal was still out there. Conner had checked in with Lex Duncan, but no new leads had turned up. "Promise me you'll go in through the front of the club, not from the alley."

"You know I have to use the stage door," she said as she ducked under the car's gull-wing door as it rose to let her out. "Lecherous Lou will have a fit if I—"

"Tell him you have a new sugar daddy who's coming to

spend lots of money in his club—but only if you walk in through the front entrance."

She rolled her eyes and pulled her garment bag from the backseat. "Sugar daddy?"

He shrugged with a grin. "Sounds better than fairy godmother."

She laughed. "You're crazy, you know that?"

Yeah, about her. "More so every minute."

He watched her walk away on the tourist-crowded sidewalk in a simple pencil skirt and blouse, and a pair of sexy, do-me shoes that should be illegal, her hips swaying enticingly. Leaving a trail of turning male heads in her wake.

He wanted to jump out of the car and strangle every one of them for looking at her that way.

Damn, he was in *such* deep trouble.

Traffic barely inched along, so he fell farther and farther behind her. For a moment he lost sight of her in the moving throng. His pulse jacked up. He didn't like this. He shouldn't have let her get out of the car. To his relief, she got stuck at a Do Not Walk sign at the next corner and actually obeyed it. Meanwhile his lane jerked forward half a block so he almost caught up with her. She didn't know it, though, and he smiled at her impatient foot tapping as she waited.

Suddenly, he noticed someone else watching her. Closely. From the sidewalk just behind her. A man. Tall, muscular, with an olive complexion, thick black hair and a furtive look about him. A *familiar* furtive look. The guy stepped closer to Vera's back. *Too* close. As the man surreptitiously checked the crowd to both sides, Conner saw high cheekbones that gave him an exotic Hispanic or maybe Native American look.

And then it struck him. It was the man who'd been arguing with Darla! In front of police headquarters!

Alarm zinged through Conner's insides. Just as Vera's

stance went straight and rigid. Slowly, she put her hands out to her sides.

Holy hell! The bastard had a gun to her back!

Conner leaped from the car and barreled down the street to her aid, knocking people aside, apologizing as he ran. It took him about seven seconds flat to reach her. They were the longest seconds of his life.

"Hey!" he yelled just before flinging himself onto the douchebag's back. "Get away from her!" A mistake. The man was quick. He spun, saw Conner and took off, just missing being tackled. Conner managed to avoid mowing down Vera, but when he veered, he slammed into the streetlight post. Stars burst in his head.

"Conner!" Her voice echoed like he was in a tunnel. "Oh, my God! Conner! Are you okay?"

He gave his head a shake to clear it as well as his hearing. "Did someone catch that guy?" he demanded, scanning the area around them. Concerned tourists looked back at him blankly.

Damn.

"That was him, wasn't it?" Vera said, obviously totally freaked out. "The guy who broke into my apartment. He had a gun, Conner! He was going to shoot me!"

The circle of tourists glanced nervously in the direction the man had run, and started to back away. Out on the street, car horns started honking.

"Damn. I left the car running down the block." He grasped her elbow firmly. "Come on. We're going back home."

She dug in her heels. "No, Conner," she protested. "I have to go to work!"

He towed her along unwillingly. "You were nearly mugged, woman! Or worse. How can you even consider—"

"I told you. I don't have a choice. I *need* my job. Please,

Conner. Let me go. He just wants the ring, and I don't have it. I'll be fine."

Silver had thought she was safe, too. Right before a thousand tons of pipe and wood had crashed down on her. She was still emotionally traumatized by the attack.

Damn it, he didn't want Vera in danger, too. But that determined look was back in her eyes. He knew he'd lose this argument. "All right. But I don't care how long it takes. You're not walking. Get in the car."

Thankfully she didn't argue but slid back into the car, if reluctantly.

"Did you get a close look at his face?" Conner asked her once he'd calmed down enough to think rationally. "Would you recognize him again?"

She shook her head. "No. I didn't dare turn around when he had his gun in my back. I didn't see his face at all. Did you?"

"Just from a distance, and I only caught a glimpse of it. But I think I've seen him before. I'll have Duncan pull video from the traffic cam." He pointed to the unobtrusive camera pointed at the intersection. "With luck, it got a good shot of him, and we can identify the bastard once and for all. At least see if he's the same guy I suspect of taking the Quetzal from police headquarters."

And hurting Silver.

And possibly murdering Candace.

"Damn it! I don't want you going to work tonight," Conner said, slamming his fist on the steering wheel. "I'll pay your salary—whatever you would have made."

She stared at him for a moment, then smiled weakly. "I know you just want to help, but…I can't do that."

"I'm not trying to buy you, Vera."

"I know that. But, no, thanks."

It took them ten minutes to drive the block and a half to

the Diamond Lounge parking lot. By the time they got out of the car and he escorted her to the stage door, she'd composed herself completely. He didn't know how she could be so calm. Or so stubborn about accepting his help. A man had just tried to kill her!

Since Conner wasn't an employee of the club, the guard wouldn't let him in the side entrance.

"Be careful," he admonished Vera, giving her a worried kiss. "I'll be in the audience all night. If you need me just yell."

She smiled and touched his cheek. "My hero."

He knew it was just teasing, but her endearment made him feel warm all over. Or maybe it was just the hot Las Vegas night wind. People had given him a lot bigger compliments, accompanied by far more substantial rewards than a smile. So why did every little thing this woman do affect him so deeply?

He made his way around to the front, directly to the head of the line of schlubs waiting to get into the exclusive club. As an Old Las Vegas landmark, the Diamond Lounge was extremely popular with tourists and locals alike. But it didn't surprise him that the bouncer immediately recognized him, either from the society pages, or because he'd been part of the stir last night.

"Evening, Mr. Rothchild. Welcome back," the brawny man said, ushering him past the velvet rope.

After paying his exorbitant cover, he was immediately shown to the same table as last night, right in front of the stage. He suppressed a chuckle of amusement. Had Vera really told them he was her sugar daddy? He wouldn't put it past her. She had a wicked sense of humor, that woman.

This time a whole bottle of champagne appeared on his table, served by a pretty petite brunette who displayed her nearly nude body invitingly for him as she poured.

He was so not interested.

A beautiful redhead came out onstage in a sexy French maid's outfit and for the next fifteen minutes did a very energetic number with the center pole. The men perched on the bar stools arranged against the edge of the stage cheered and groaned in approval.

Conner drained a glass of champagne and was actually bored. He was only interested in seeing one certain, particular woman take off her clothes. And the thought of her doing it in front of all these clowns was making him want to swallow the whole damned bottle.

He checked his watch. Eight-thirty.

Vera didn't come on until eleven.

Hell. It was going to be a really, really long night.

He was out there.

Conner.

Why did the thought of that one man being in the audience put butterflies in Vera's stomach and impossible feelings in her heart? Feelings of warmth and affection, and sadness and regret, all balled up in one giant knot?

She was falling in love with the man. That's why.

Despair filled Vera as she prepared to go out onstage. For the first time ever, she didn't want to do this. Wished she'd chosen a more conventional means of making a living. Hadn't let a thousand men see her wearing nothing more than a G-string.

Stop it! she told herself.

There was nothing wrong with what she did. And it wasn't as though she'd had a lot of choice.

As Jerry the stagehand pulled back the curtain for her, she thought about all the times she'd strutted out onstage and enjoyed the heck out of it. She'd loved the power of her female body over the punters. Loved the effect she'd had on them, reducing strong, intelligent men to blithering bundles of testosterone willing to give her everything they had for just one more peek. Loved that she was giving a thrill to those who had no one, and to those with someone waiting for them a reason to go home and give that woman a thrill of her own.

And then she thought of Conner, out there, waiting for her to come out and perform. How terrifying was that? Because suddenly she realized there was nothing she wanted more than to have him take her home and give *her* a thrill.

She was nothing if not realistic. She knew a man like him would never love her back. But that didn't mean she couldn't enjoy him while he still wanted her. And he did want her. Anyone with eyes could see that.

So why was she wasting time? The man was out there, waiting, needing to be seduced. Quickly. Before Agent Duncan found Darla and the Quetzal-crazed maniac, and Vera had to go back to her old life.

This life.

Without Conner.

The long chords of her organ music started. Her cue.

She fluffed the skirt of her faux wedding gown and gave her breasts an extra push up.

Okay. This was it.

The man didn't stand a chance. When she was done with this performance, he'd be putty in her hands.

At least for a little while. Longer if she was lucky. Until life intervened and he came to his senses.

But in the meantime he'd be hers. All hers.

Her very own Prince Charming.

For one magical night.

Chapter 10

Conner sat back in his seat, exhaled a long, long, *long* breath and willed the goose bumps running up and down his arms to go away.

His body was painfully aroused, throbbing hard and craving satisfaction.

The woman was a witch, pure and simple. She'd bewitched him. Again. Totally. Thoroughly. Unabashedly. She'd danced her dance of the seven veils with that gossamer white wedding costume, and he'd been as lost as King Herod, ready to throw whatever she wished at her feet. Money. Fame. His heart on a platter.

Damn. How pathetically cliché was this? Rich man falling for a much younger stripper, willing to alienate his family, his friends, his entire social circle, to be with her.

How could he even consider it?

He'd be on the front page of every tabloid, laughed at

behind his back. His career would suffer. His family would be embarrassed. Probably end up being disowned by his overly socially conscious father.

All because he suddenly couldn't imagine his life without Vera Mancuso in it.

And yet, there it was.

He wanted her anyway.

He wanted her.

But he just couldn't. Couldn't do that to his family. Couldn't toss aside everything he'd worked so hard to achieve.

There had to be another way.

A way to have her, all to himself, but not expose either of them to the severe downsides of a relationship like theirs.

Relationship.

He shuddered, and even more goose bumps broke out on his flesh. What was he *thinking?* There must be a—

"Mr. Rothchild?"

With a start, he came back to the present. Vera had left the stage ages ago, and another girl had replaced her. Ever since, he'd just been staring into space, his mind whirling in a chaos of growing panic.

He turned to see a middle-aged man with an obviously expensive but still oddly ill-fitting suit standing by his table. "Yes?"

The man extended his hand. "I'm Lou Majors, the manager, Mr. Rothchild. Welcome to the Diamond Lounge."

Ah. If it wasn't Lecherous Lou himself. Conner projected his voice over the bass-heavy stripper music blaring from the loudspeakers, "Thank you. Won't you join me?" It never hurt to schmooze the enemy.

"Don't mind if I do." The manager snapped his fingers at a hostess, who hurried over with another bottle of champagne. This time it was Cristal. Nice.

Also pretty nervy, because Conner was the one who'd end

up paying for it. Not that he cared. Beat the hell out of the cheap stuff he'd been drinking.

"Enjoying the floor show?" Lou asked politely, leaning in so he could be heard.

"Absolutely. Some parts more than others." Conner sent him a knowing, male-bonding-type smile.

Lou smiled back amiably. "Couldn't help but notice. You're acquainted with Miss LaRue, I take it?"

LaRue? Oh, right. Vera's stage name. "Yes. Met her here, actually. Yesterday."

At the reminder of the disruption, a shadow of annoyance passed through the manager's eyes but was quickly gone. "Her lawyer, I take it."

Conner winked lasciviously and leaned in closer. "Who could resist?" May as well go for broke. If the scumbucket thought she had a wealthy protector, he'd never dare fire her. "But I'm no longer her lawyer. I passed her case to a colleague." He lowered his voice, confidential-like. "Conflict of interest, if you get my drift."

He did. Lou couldn't have looked more pleased if Conner'd just handed him a stack of hundred-dollar bills. Which no doubt was exactly what the old roué had in mind. "I see." Several seconds went by as the manager regarded Conner. Finally he said, "Mr. Rothchild, I have a very special offer to make you."

"Yeah? What's that?"

Lou beckoned, rose and led him through the club to the sweeping red-carpeted staircase that led upstairs. On the way up, he refilled his champagne flute and handed it back. "I think you'll be very interested in this unique opportunity."

They ducked into the same VIP room as yesterday. Conner raised a brow questioningly. "What's this all about?"

Lou cleared his throat. "Are you the kind of man who likes…private parties, Mr. Rothchild?"

His brows rose higher. "That depends on who's invited."

"Men such as yourself. Wealthy. Discriminating. Discreet."

Suddenly, it hit him. *Good Lord.* If this was going where he thought it was going, the Parker case just got a huge break. "Go on."

"The ladies are of the highest caliber, of course. Only the best, most beautiful women are in attendance. Women who will cater to your every whim."

Lou looked at him expectantly, the man's crude excitement coming through loud and clear. Whether it was excitement over the prospect of the power he wielded over helpless beautiful women, or the prospect of all the money Conner would have to spend to attend that shindig, he couldn't guess. Suzie Parker had told him the attendees paid five thousand dollars each for an invitation to these exclusive gentlemen's house parties.

But Conner was a very, very rich man. He could get any woman he wanted for no more than the cost of a drink. His reputation was well-known.

He shrugged, playing it cool. "There's only one woman I'm interested in catering to me," he said, feigning indifference to the whole thing. "And I've been told in no uncertain terms she doesn't do private parties. Of any kind."

Lou's eyes narrowed, his lip curling. After a brief pause, he said, "What if I could change her mind?"

Whoops. Not the direction Conner'd meant to go. He scrambled for a reason to refuse, but Lou beat him to the draw.

"I'll make you a deal. If she'll do a party here in the VIP room with you, you'll give my other invitation a try." Because he was so sure after one visit, Conner'd be sucked into the decadence.

Hell, that's what a man got for cultivating his reputation as a player and a heartbreaker all over town. Which, ironically enough, he'd done in order to *avoid* breaking hearts. He'd never been interested in hanging with one woman for more than a few days.

Before now.

Temptation loomed large. On both counts.

This was an unprecedented opportunity to help Suzie Parker by witnessing firsthand what she'd been forced to do. To gather hard evidence against the culprits running these parties and shut them down for good. So other innocent girls weren't caught in the trap, lured by the money into selling themselves short.

Not to mention being able to have Vera all to himself in the VIP room, driving him crazy with her delectable body, dancing up close and personal.

Except she'd be madder than a coyote if Lou made her do it. She'd probably never speak to Conner again.

Which could, of course, solve that other problem. The one where he was about to throw away his whole life to have her. No sense doing that if she wasn't even speaking to him.

He hesitated. Just long enough for Lou to pull out his cell phone and make a three-word call. "Send her up."

Oh, crap.

Vera was sitting at the dressing-room mirror touching up her makeup and listening to Tawni prattle on about some man she'd just met. Some computer IT guy from New Orleans.

"Always wanted to visit the Big Easy," Tawni said. "Do you think I should go?"

"Is he married?" Vera asked.

Tawni flung out a hand. "Who cares? We're not talking about having the guy's kid, here, just a little fling!"

"Which can lead to all sorts of heartache for everyone involved, especially if he's married," Vera pointed out. "I'd ask before I even considered it."

Tawni sighed. "I suppose you're right. Wouldn't want to have my eyes scratched out by some dumb punter's irate wife."

"Very sensible."

"What about your guy?"

"I have no guy."

Tawni snorted. "Yeah? Then who was Mr. Tall, Rich and Handsome in the front row drooling into his champagne? For the second night in a row, I might add. The one whose ten-million-dollar mansion you happen to be staying at?"

Vera swiveled on her stool to face her friend. "We haven't slept together." Well. Not technically. It didn't count when only one of the parties got off and there was no bed involved. Right?

Tawni's eyes bugged out. "Are you *insane?* What are you waiting for?"

Vera sighed dreamily. "Nothing, anymore. I decided to seduce him tonight."

"Good plan," Tawni said in exasperation. "Jeez, girl, the man is worth megabucks. You've got to hurry up and soak him for all he's worth!"

She shook her head, feeling a loopy smile spread on her face. "No. I couldn't. It's not like that. He likes me. Respects me."

Tawni slapped her hands to the sides of her face. "Are you out of your mind? *Respects* you? Look at yourself in the mirror, Vera May Mancuso. Does that look like the sort of woman a man has any kind of honorable thoughts about? Mark my words, he's after something you've got, but it ain't R-E-S-P-E-C-T."

"Maybe. Maybe not. It doesn't matter. I've decided to give it to him anyway."

Something in her voice must have given her away. Tawni gasped. "Oh, sweet heaven. You're *in love* with the man! My God, girl, you just met him yesterday!"

"I know. Totally insane, isn't it? I took one look at him, and it was like…like I'd been zapped by a magic wand or some-thing. Bells rang. Stars exploded." Or maybe that part was just the stage lights reflecting off the incredible ring she'd been wearing. The Tears of the Quetzal. She'd been blinded by its hypnotic brilliance. No wonder some lunatic had become obsessed by it.

Tawni was still staring at her incredulously.

Vera held up a hand. "I know. I'm certifiable. Believe me, I wasn't going to touch him—" much "—but oh, God, Tawni, I want him. I want to feel what it's like to be with him. Just once. Don't worry, I'm not fool enough to think it'll last."

Sympathy filled Tawni's gaze. "Oh, sweetie, you do have it bad. Come here, girl." She stretched out her arms, and Vera went into them, grateful for a hug, grateful for a friend who knew exactly what she was going through. No matter how jaded they pretended to be, their hearts still broke like everyone else's.

"You're right, sweetie," Tawni murmured. "Don't you worry about the future. You go for it. Get all the loving you can out of him. Just hang on to that precious heart of yours. Don't you give that to any man, you hear?"

Vera nodded. "I won't."

But it was too late, and they both knew it.

Still, she told herself, at least she'd have some amazing memories.

She pulled back from Tawni's hug, filling with a jittery kind of excitement. She really *was* going to go for it.

Jerry poked his head in the door just then. "Miss LaRue?"

She looked up, surprised. She wasn't on again for another two hours. "Yeah, Jerry?"

"Lecherous Lou wants to see you. Upstairs. Room seven."

Now what? Lou knew she was absolutely adamant— Okay, wait. Maybe… "Do you know if there's anyone with him?" she asked Jerry.

"That rich dude's been panting after your bod."

Excellent. "Tell him I'll be there in a minute." Jerry left. She met Tawni's I-told-you-so gaze in the mirror. "Don't say a word. Not a blessed word."

"Did I say anything? Here, look, this is me not saying a single damn thing." Tawni made a zipping motion over her lips as Vera gathered her skirts and headed out the door. "You go get 'im, girl," she called after her. "Make the boy wish he'd never been born with that thing between his legs."

That was the whole idea. For now. But later, after they went home, she'd make him glad again. Oh, so very, very glad.

And her, too.

"There you are, my dear," Lecherous Lou said when she swept into the VIP room.

Conner was standing next to him, looking too handsome for his own good. Damn, the man was fine, as Tawni would say. Broad shoulders; square jaw; long, hard, muscular legs; strong hands. And those eyes. She'd never known eyes so bone-quiveringly sexy as those hot-as-the-desert hazel ones gazing at her from under his perfectly shaped masculine brows. "Vera," he said in greeting.

"Hello, Mr. Rothchild," she said with demure formality. "Lou. What can I do for you gentlemen?"

"I think you know what Mr. Rothchild would like, Vera," Lou said. Subtlety had never been his strong suit.

She allowed herself a coy smile at her would-be lover. "I'm pretty sure that would be illegal. Wouldn't want to get any of us into trouble with the law, would we?"

Those perfect brows flicked. She'd caught him by surprise. He'd been expecting her to flatly refuse, as she had yesterday.

"Of course not!" Lou blustered. "Nothing illegal. Just a standard lap dance, that's all. The VS1 Special."

Which was code for total nudity.

She swallowed.

She'd avoided this for so long that the words almost stuck in her throat. "All right," she said.

Omigod, what was she doing?

What they both wanted. That's what.

Lou almost fell over. He'd been expecting a total refusal, too, and to have to threaten her with her job. "Get lost," she told him. "Before I change my mind."

He was out the soundproof door, and the gauzy curtains were drawn closed faster than she could blink.

"Surprised?" she asked Conner when they were alone.

The lingering shock and the slight parting of his lips belied his causal stance. "I could have sworn you don't do lap dances."

"This isn't a lap dance."

"Strange. I'm pretty sure that's what you just agreed to."

She smiled. And took a step toward him. "Then, it'll be our little secret—" and another step "—what we really do."

That's when he started to get nervous. And in spite of himself, excited. She could see his body reacting to the fantasies in his mind. The ones she'd planted there. "Vera? What's going on?"

"I hope you're prepared, Mr. Rothchild," she said, lowering her voice to a throaty purr, and with one finger pushed him backward onto the divan. "To be seduced."

Chapter 11

Vera seduced him slowly, minute by minute, inch by inch, the way she'd done onstage earlier. If Conner had any notion of resisting her, the man could just forget it.

She was an expert at very few things, but this was one of them. She knew how to make a man want her.

Not that he needed any help in that department. He'd made no secret of his desire to sleep with her. He hadn't pressed her on it, but only because she'd told him no. The man was a true gentleman, just as he'd said.

And now he would get his reward.

Well. Sort of. She knew he'd do his damnedest to follow club rules and not touch her. It would be pure torture on him. Heck, for both of them. But it would make the coming night all the sweeter, once they got back to his place.

She adjusted the music to a low, bluesy song she loved, and took her place in the middle of the small room. He sat sprawled on the divan, looking like a tiger who couldn't quite believe a kitten had wandered into his cage.

"You don't have to do this," he said.

Making her fall for him all the more.

"I want to," she assured him. "Just relax and enjoy the show."

"I already did. You were incredible onstage. It felt like I was the only man in the room and you were dancing just for me."

"You were." She smiled and started to sway her hips to the music. "And I was."

His eyes darkened, his smile going sexy. "What brought on the change of heart?"

"You," she said simply. And let her body take over.

She knew all the moves, but suddenly they had a whole new meaning for her. She wanted to seduce this man, body and soul. Wanted to entice him. Enthrall him. Make him pant. Make him sweat. Make him never, ever forget this dance of temptation…

Or her.

Slowly, she peeled off her wedding gown. Taking her time. Moving her body to the music. Teasing him. Provoking him. Making the anticipation last and last. Until she was left wearing only the lace corset, stockings and shoes. The G-string of tiny seed pearls she'd selected for tonight hardly counted as attire.

His gaze devoured her, lingering on the special wax job her line of work demanded.

"Like what you see?"

"I'd like it a whole lot better closer up."

She smiled. "Yeah?"

He looked relaxed, arms lying along the back cushions of the sofa, his legs spread wide. But she knew it was a hard-won facade. There was a film of sweat on his forehead that had nothing to do with the outside night heat, and the pulse on the side of his throat throbbed wildly. Not to mention that solid ridge in the front of his pants. "Oh, yeah."

She moved closer. He swallowed.

He couldn't touch, but there were no such restrictions on her. She put a knee to each side of his, kneeling on the red leather divan with her hands on his shoulders, and straddled his lower thighs. Keeping distance between them.

"This better?" she asked.

"Not nearly close enough," he murmured darkly.

The fabric of his suit was smooth and luxurious, cool to the touch. But the man in it was sizzling. She ran her fingers down his shirtfront. "Mmm. You're hot," she observed.

"Burning up," he agreed.

She peeled off his jacket and tossed it aside. Loosened his tie.

"Take it off," he ordered huskily.

"Why, Mr. Rothchild…"

"The tie."

She obliged, using the length of silk like a sex toy. Drawing it off slowly, teasing him with the end, glancing at his wrist debating whether to tie him up to the iron ring attached to the wall above his head.

"Don't even think about it," he warned.

She smiled, setting it aside. "Later, then."

"We'll see about that."

One by one, she teased his shirt buttons open. Touched his broad chest. Reveled in the feel of his skin under her fingers. In the soft scratch of the curls of masculine hair. He shifted under her, and she could feel the slight trembling of his thighs.

She wet her lips and brushed them over his. He groaned softly. "You're killing me here, you know that."

She put her hands to his chest, rubbed her thumbs over his tight nipples. "Hope you have nine lives."

He sucked in a breath, lifted his knees and tipped her into his chest. "Not fair," he gasped.

She tilted her head up, taking her time pulling her body away from his. "Who said anything about fair?"

He gave a strangled laugh. "Witch."

"Candy-ass."

"You are so getting a spanking when we get home."

She winked. "Promises, promises."

His eyes cut down to hers, darkened to the color of a forest in a storm. "You are a naughty girl."

"Want to see how naughty?" she whispered in his ear.

"I'm your lawyer. I need to know these things."

Her corset was held together in front by a row of bows. She reached down, found the end of one of the ribbons, and tugged it almost open. Then she put the ribbon to his lips. With a jerk of his head, he finished the job. Her breasts spilled out of the garment…just enough to be a tease.

She lifted up on her knees a little. Like lightning he grasped the end of the next ribbon with his teeth and tugged that one open, too. Her breasts tumbled out, brushing his face. He groaned, trying to catch a nipple with his tongue and teeth.

"Uh-uh," she scolded, wagging a finger. Feeling the intimate contact like a wave of shivers.

"Let me," he pleaded.

"Finish undoing the bows. Then we'll see."

His hot breath puffed over her skin, his wet tongue grazed her flesh as he bent to his task. Her nipples spiraled harder. Achy coils of desire tightened around her center.

He made quick work of the bows. Clever man. The corset slid to the floor. On impulse, she unclasped her G-string and let it slither off, too. She wanted to be completely naked for him.

His expression was pure sin as his gaze caressed her.

"You are so damn beautiful," he whispered.

Still up on her knees, she bent forward, offering him her breasts. She wanted to feel his mouth on her. He latched on like a hungry babe, suckling one then the other, until she was panting with need.

With a groan, she pulled herself away. "Any more and I'll come," she murmured.

"Do it," he urged. "I want to see you come apart for me again."

"Not here." She eased out a shuddering breath.

He blinked and glanced around, as though he'd completely forgotten where they were. He'd dug his fingers deep into the divan back, holding on to the cushions with a death grip, but now he eased them off and flexed them. "God. You're right. What was I thinking?" He nuzzled his lips against her throat. "Let's get out of here."

"I still have another show."

"Forget it. You're coming home with me." He stood up, sweeping her into his arms. *"Now."*

She didn't protest, other than to insist on picking up her discarded costume and his jacket and tie. He and Lecherous Lou seemed to have some kind of understanding. Hopefully she wouldn't lose her job over this.

Not that it would change her mind if she did. She was ready to be his. In every way. More than ready.

Conner drove like a madman, making the trip to his house in less than twelve minutes. He didn't want to waste a single second. He wanted to be inside her, now, finding release for this volcano of desire roiling inside his body.

Before leaving the club, he'd allowed her to slip back into her pencil skirt, peasant blouse and do-me shoes, but nothing else. He could see her tawny nipples through the almost-sheer fabric of the blouse. He was dying. He needed her under him.

As soon as they got inside the door of his mansion, he had her up against the wall, his mouth to her breast. She moaned, clasping his head in her hands, pulling him closer.

"Conner," she pleaded, her voice strangled, writhing against the wall as he ground the silk blouse onto her nipple with his wet tongue.

"I'm here, baby." He threw aside his jacket and practically ripped the buttons from his shirt, ridding himself of it. She lifted her shirt up over her ample breasts, baring them for him. They were breasts a man could lose himself in. Soft, round, full. Perfect.

He could smell the feminine scent of her desire, lightly musky and spicy, an alluring aphrodisiac that made him twitch in an agony of want.

With a growl, he banded his arms around her and carried her into the living room, swept the things off a low coffee table, and lowered her onto her back on it. Wrenching her legs apart, he tasted her, covering her with his mouth and tongue.

She gasped, arched and splintered apart. So fast he didn't have time to enjoy it. So he did it again.

When he finally climbed up on the table and lowered himself on top of her, she was totally wrung out and he was ready to detonate. He grasped under her knees and spread them.

"Protection?" she managed to murmur.

"Taken care of," he told her. Thank God he'd tucked a few condoms in his trouser pocket. Just in case.

"Mmm."

He thrust into her. The feel of her hot flesh surrounding him burst through his consciousness like a kaleidoscope of erotic sensation. He froze. If he moved a muscle he'd be lost. She held him tight, her chest expanding and contracting against him. It wasn't helping. He groaned.

"Conner?"

"Yeah, babe?"

"Is anything wrong?"

"Other than me being about to shame myself and totally ruin my macho reputation?"

She let out a surprised laugh. Her muscles contracted around him.

Jeez-uz.

"Baby, have mercy," he begged.

Her eyes softened, joy suffusing her whole face. She was so lovely his breath caught in his lungs. Was it really possible *he* had done that to her? Made her so happy she glowed with it?

"Kiss me," she whispered.

So he did. Long and wet and thorough as a spring downpour in the Mojave. She wrapped her legs around his waist and held him tight and used her heels on his backside to push him deep, deep, deep into her. So deep he found he couldn't hold back.

"It's okay. Let yourself go," she whispered into his mouth, her voice low and thready with emotion.

He shuddered, fighting it. Not wanting it to be over so quickly. "Too soon," he gritted out.

"We have all night," she refuted breathily.

Which was a good thing, because he had no more strength to resist.

An overwhelming surge of pleasure crashed over him. And he surrendered. Surrendered to the carnal bliss. Surrendered to the emotional rightness. Surrendered to the deep inner knowledge that after this night, he would never be the same man again.

This was just the beginning.

Chapter 12

"No, Dad. Because I don't—" Speaking on the phone, Conner did not look like a happy camper. In fact, he looked downright angry. "What about Mike? Why can't he—"

Vera wrapped the silk robe Conner'd lent her a bit tighter around her body and sank a bit deeper into the leather recliner she was curled into, trying to make herself invisible. They were in his study while he'd put out a fire or two at work. This didn't sound like work, though.

"Yes, Dad. Of course I am. But—"

They'd made love all night. And all morning. And half the afternoon. They'd shared passions and done things together she'd never done with another human being. He'd claimed her body; she'd given him her heart and her soul.

But she still felt like a trespasser in his world.

"Fine, Dad. Yes, I understand." He slammed the phone down with a curse, a scowl etched on his face.

She didn't dare ask him what was wrong. Not her place.

"Too early for a drink?" she ventured. It was just past four. Hell, it was five o'clock just down the road in Denver. At least she thought it was. Of course, one never knew with Mountain Time.

He looked up, apparently surprised to see her sitting there. *Oops.* Should have kept her mouth shut.

"Come here," he ordered.

She untangled her legs and did as he bid. Normally she wasn't such a "yes" girl, but last night she'd quickly realized the considerable benefits of doing as he asked.

He patted the desk blotter in front of him, and she duly climbed up and sat.

"Open your robe."

She smiled. The man was truly insatiable. Okay, this she could do. Her body already quickening, she unbelted the robe and held it open in anticipation of whatever he had in mind to make himself forget the conversation he'd just had with his father.

He didn't touch her. Just looked. And looked.

"You have the body of a goddess," he finally said. "You could have any man you want at the charity ball tonight."

"Why would I want anyone else when I have you?" she asked, reaching out for his hand and raising it to her cheek. She kissed his palm. He frowned.

She knew it was the wrong thing to do. Men didn't like it when a woman got all clingy after sex. But she just couldn't help herself.

Heart on her sleeve? Look it up. Her picture would be right there under the definition.

Did she care?

Ask her tomorrow.

She brought his hand to her breast. He cupped her,

running his thumb gently over the nipple. Shivers of pleasure went up her spine.

"And you make love like a god," she murmured.

Abruptly, he rolled his chair forward and leaned her backward onto his arm, bracing her as he took her other nipple in his mouth. Using his tongue, he imitated what his thumb was doing to the first one.

She sucked in a sharp breath, already rushing toward climax. Her body had gotten so tuned to him, physically, all it took was a touch or a kiss and she was practically there.

He withdrew, kissing her on the mouth instead. A sweet, tender kiss.

Her stomach sank.

A goodbye kiss.

Momentarily stunned, her heart squeezed painfully. Wow. That had happened more quickly than she'd thought.

But okay. She was a big girl. She could handle it.

She steadied herself, physically and mentally, for the inevitable.

"Are you ready for the ball?" he asked. "You still okay with what you have to do?"

The question caught her off guard.

In between their lovemaking and occasional foraging trips from the bedroom to the kitchen, they'd talked about what she would do tonight, how she'd go about getting the information about Darla that they needed. How to lure Darla's accomplices in the jewelry theft ring out into the open. *Alleged* accomplices.

Vera was still convinced Darla was innocent. But she'd sworn to do her best for Conner and she would. She'd rather know the truth about her sister, either way.

"Of course," she answered. She was nervous as hell about it but ready as ever. She thought about that phone call. "Why? Has something happened?"

His gaze dropped to her breasts again, and he stroked his hands over them possessively. "No," he said. "Nothing that affects anything important."

Now, there was a nonanswer if ever she'd heard one.

"What was that argument with your father all about, Conner?" she asked, a sick foreboding knotting in her stomach. "What did he want?"

Her lover leaned over and pressed his lips to her abdomen, trailing down to her belly button. He flicked his tongue into it. "Nothing important," he repeated.

Which probably meant it was. So important he didn't want to tell her. Which probably meant she wouldn't like it, whatever it was.

His tongue trailed lower still. "Spread your legs."

"Conner—"

"Open them."

He was definitely trying to distract her.

It was working.

She moaned as his tongue slipped between her folds, still swollen from hours of lovemaking. It felt warm and silky on her tender flesh. *So good.*

Ah, well. She'd find out soon enough what the problem was. No sense borrowing trouble.

Meanwhile, she planned to enjoy every minute she had left with him. And this was a very, very good start.

He had to tell her.

Consumed with guilt—and fury at his meddling father— Conner helped Vera into the white stretch limo he'd ordered to take them to the Lights of Las Vegas Charity Ball.

She looked like a princess in the strapless sapphire-blue satin gown he'd selected for her tonight. Worldly, sophisticated, stunning. He wanted her to be on his arm. All evening.

So there'd be no possibility of other men charming her, dancing with her, tempting her away.

Unfortunately, that was not to be. Dear old Dad had unknowingly made certain of it.

The old bugger'd be even more delighted if he actually knew what he'd done. Conner's father was a stand-up guy, but completely unreasonable when it concerned the family's reputation. Dad had tolerated Conner's rakish behavior— barely—up until now only because he was young, single and male. But he couldn't imagine Michael Rothchild ever in a million years condoning his son taking a stripper to a high-profile social event like this one. Much less dating one. No matter how amazing a person she was. Or how incredibly gorgeous.

Conner took his place beside her in the limo and tucked her under his arm. She nestled against him, resting her hand on his thigh.

"Nervous?" he asked.

She nodded. "Terrified."

"Don't be. You'll do fine. And you look exquisite."

She smiled up at him as she had so often today. Happy. Trusting. "Thank you." Her long lashes swept shyly downward, making his heart squeeze.

"You take my breath away, Vera Mancuso," he said and gave her a lingering kiss.

"The feeling's mutual, Conner Rothchild," she whispered.

He reached into his pocket for the velvet pouch he'd had his secretary deliver to the house that afternoon. From it he pulled a solid gold Byzantine rope necklace that had been his grandmother's. "I thought this would go nicely with your dress."

"Oh, Conner, it's beautiful!" she exclaimed, fingering it reverently after he'd fastened it around her neck. "But—"

"There's more."

When he pulled out the ring, her eyes went wide as saucers. "My God! Where did you get that? I thought the Tears of the Quetzal was stolen!"

He slipped it on her finger.

"It's a copy. Paste. The thief left it in place of the original when he stole that from police evidence. Not sure how he got hold of this one. It was supposedly in my aunt's jewelry box in her bedroom. My grandfather had it made decades ago for family members to wear out in public. Before he decided the ring was cursed and locked it away for good in a vault somewhere. Anyway, LVMPD turned over the paste ring to the FBI, too, and Duncan said we could borrow it tonight, thinking its appearance might help lure the thieves."

Conner had debated long and hard with himself about this. Having Vera wear the fake Quetzal could potentially put her in danger from the psycho thief. But as long as she only wore it at the ball, where security would be ultratight, and went home with him afterward, she should be safe. It also reassured him knowing that Duncan would have his men watching his property all night, too.

As an extra precaution, Conner had hired a bodyguard to discreetly follow her around at the ball, because Conner wouldn't be able to watch over her personally.

She held her fingers up to the limo's overhead light. Even in the dim wattage, the faux chameleon diamond shot off a shower of purple and green sparks, almost like the genuine article. "Wow. If I hadn't had the real thing on my own finger, I'd sure be fooled. It's nearly identical."

"Not many could tell the difference," he agreed.

Just then, the limo made a turn into a circular driveway. Damn. His time was up.

Vera peered out the tinted windows at the private mansion they'd pulled up in front of. "Where are we?" she asked.

"My brother's house," Conner said, steeling himself to meet her eyes. "We're picking him up, along with his date. And mine."

She did her best to hide her visceral reaction, but he clearly saw the flash of shock and devastation in her eyes before she managed to mask them. Her lips parted, then closed. "Your…date?"

Damn his father. "The daughter of an important client. She flew in from Paris yesterday and—"

Vera held up her hand. "No, it's okay," she said, though she couldn't quite squelch the strain in her voice. "You don't have to explain. We agreed I'd be coming as your assistant, not date. It's more believable this way."

So much for happy and trusting.

"Vera—" He reached for her, but she scooted away, all the way to the other side of the limo. He moved to go after her.

"Don't," she said, just as the door opened.

He halted, torn. She was his lover. He should never have let his father bully him into this farce. And yet…there was a microscopic part of him that was secretly relieved not to have to reveal their relationship just yet—and bear the brunt of social and familial disapproval.

He was such a damn coward.

"Howdy, bro," his brother, Mike, stuck his head in the door that had been opened by the chauffeur and greeted him. "Hey, now, what have we here?" Mike's confusion was obvious when he spotted Vera sitting in the corner. Then he really looked at her, and his face lit up. "A threesome? You dirty old man, you."

Mike, or Michael Rothchild Jr., was the older brother, but acted like a kid sometimes. He had no emotional radar.

"Just get in the damn car," Conner said evenly.

Mike stepped aside and his striking blond fiancée, Audra, slid into the seat opposite Conner. She leaned over and air-kissed him on the cheek. "Hi, Conner. Good to see y—" She also spotted Vera and halted in mid-word. "Hello," she said, glancing between her and Conner. "This is, um, interesting."

"My assistant, Vera Mancuso." Conner cut off her blatant rampant speculation. She was as bad as his brother. The perfect pair. "Vera's helping me with a case tonight."

Audra's brows rose delicately. But she refrained from comment, because Conner's date had just glided onto the seat next to him. She was model-thin with shiny black hair and long legs exposed by a slit running up the side of her gown. *Way* up. Aristocratic features, olive skin, a long neck and slim arms dripping with jewelry. The woman oozed class and sophistication.

His father knew him well. She was just his type.

Up until two days ago.

She raised her hand, European style. "Annabella Pruitt," she said in a cultured voice. *"Enchanté."*

He knew he was expected to kiss her hand, but he couldn't make himself do it. He shook it awkwardly instead, introducing himself, trying to subtly ease his body closer to Vera, who sat primly on the other side of him, maintaining a perfectly blank face.

"Did I hear you say assistant?" Mike queried after he'd climbed in and gotten settled next to Audra. He smiled at Vera when Conner introduced her to him and Annabella. "Just like my little brother to be working a case on a night like this," he said with good-humored disapproval.

"That's why he brought me," Vera said smoothly, the first peep she'd uttered. "So he wouldn't have to work. Now he can devote all his time to his lovely date." She smiled genially at the other woman, but Conner knew better than to think he'd been forgiven.

"Now *that's* a waste of a beautiful woman," Mike

remarked disgustedly, and Audra smacked him in the arm—but there was no heat in it. "So what kind of case does one work at a fancy ball?" he asked, patently intrigued by the whole situation.

"The confidential kind," Conner interrupted before Vera could answer. He sat back and folded his arms over his chest irritatedly. This was *so* not the night he'd envisioned.

Audra hadn't taken her curious eyes off Vera. "I didn't know Conner had hired an assistant," she ventured. "You're very young. Are you a junior associate in the firm? Paralegal maybe?"

"Confidential informant." Conner cut off whatever Vera'd opened her mouth to say. "She knows people."

"You do look familiar," Mike said with a curious tilt of his head. "Have we met somewhere? At another charity event perhaps?"

Vera's glued-on smile didn't waver. "You probably know my sister, Darla St. Giles."

Mike's brows shot into his scalp. "Good God. Darla has a sister? How did I not know that?"

"Vera isn't into Darla's social whirl," Conner supplied.

"I prefer to stay out of the tabloids." She folded her hands in her lap.

And that's when Mike noticed the fake ring on her finger. His eyes bugged out, and his shocked gaze snapped to Conner.

Annabella apparently noticed it, too. "What an unusual ring you have," she said. "May I see it?"

"Of course," Vera said, and held out her hand. Annabella let it rest on her fingers as she examined it. Over his lap. His brother peered at him over their fingers. Conner peered back, grinding his jaw.

"Extraordinary. Where on earth did you get it?" Annabella asked.

"Why," Vera said innocently. So innocently he knew he was

in trouble the second the word left her mouth. "From your date." Her lips smiled up at him, but her eyes were shooting daggers. "Conner gave it to me earlier tonight."

Chapter 13

She pretended she was onstage.

That was the only way she could get through this. Being onstage gave her permission to be someone else: a brave, confident woman whose power came from deep within her. Not the terrified, heartbroken, barely hanging on woman she really was.

She could do this.

She *had* to do this.

The thought of everyone's shock in the limo when she'd announced Conner had given her the Tears of the Quetzal gave her the boost she needed to pull this off. They'd naturally all jumped to the same wrong conclusion. Oddly enough, Conner hadn't corrected it. He'd actually glanced at her just as surprised as the others, but she could have sworn she'd seen him hide an amused smirk. Anyway, she'd set them straight herself, five seconds later, by adding, "For the investigation, of course!" in an innocent exclamation. But those five seconds had been glorious.

What. Ever. Now she was on her own, Conner having wandered off with his glamorous date, leaving Vera standing alone in the middle of a huge ballroom full of high-society mucky-mucks. And the uneasy feeling that someone was watching her. Conner had warned her to be on the lookout for the man who'd attacked her on the street. Thank you *so* much for that.

Damn, she needed a drink.

"Darla?" A surprised male voice assaulted her. "Is that you, babe?"

This one, at least, didn't sound dangerous.

She turned. Nor did he look like the Hispanic guy from the fuzzy traffic cam photo—but that was fairly useless. He was a raffish man about her own age, all decked out in the latest trendy Eurotrash style, blond hair going every which way.

"No," she said, taking a breath of relief and putting on her brightest smile. "I'm Vera, her roommate. Have you seen her by any chance?"

"Wow. You sure look like her. I'm Gabe. No, I haven't…"

And so it started. If she thought she'd be left alone, she'd totally misjudged Darla's friends. They might be wild and crazy, but they circled wagons for one of their own. She'd met some of them at the apartment already, so she wasn't totally out to sea. They took her under their wing, pulling her along with the flow as they made the social rounds, laughing, dancing and speculating madly with her over where Darla could have disappeared to this time. No one was worried about Darla. While everyone remarked on her ring, and a few had even read the newspaper reports that linked the ring to Candace Rothchild's murder, no one seemed overly interested in it other than as a ghoulish souvenir of that tragedy.

Unique, expensive jewels with a history were a way of life for these people. And everyone had on their most unique and expensive pieces for tonight's ball. Hers was just one more fabulous diamond to admire, gossip about, then forget.

And speaking of forgetting…she didn't think about Conner more than once, all night.

Okay, once a minute, all night.

But she was proud of the fact that she didn't track him all over the ballroom, keeping tabs on his movements, how many drinks he had, how many times he danced with that bitc—er, date, or if he ever looked across the room, searching for Vera.

She *so* didn't care.

At least, that's what she kept telling herself.

Once a minute, all night.

"Ms. Mancuso?"

She almost choked on her drink. Despite the uneventful evening so far, she'd still had the creepy feeling someone had been watching her the whole time. But probably not this guy.

A tall, elegantly dressed man with salt-and-pepper hair, who looked so much like Conner he could only be his father, or uncle, gazed down at her pleasantly.

"Y-yes," she stammered, all her hard-won poise and confidence vanishing in a fell swoop.

He extended his hand. "I'm Michael Rothchild. I understand you came with my son tonight."

Oh, God. More than once, she thought with half-hysterical irreverence. And last night, too.

She blinked, frozen by the howlingly inappropriate thought, with her hand in his. The one with the ring on it. *His* ring. "Um. Yes. But, uh, not as— I mean, I'm just working—"

He glanced at the fake Quetzal, then up again. "I just wanted to thank you." At her deer-in-the-headlights look, he added, "for helping with—" he glanced around "—well, you know." She did. She was just surprised *he* did. "Your discretion is appreciated."

"My, um—" She was about to say "pleasure," but it wasn't really, was it? So she just let the inane half comment hang there.

"*Greatly* appreciated." Michael Rothchild was still holding her hand. So firmly she couldn't politely extract it. He kept looking at her, taking in her whole person, expensive outfit and all, and it was like he saw straight through her charade. "I don't approve of your sister," he said. "but I respect family loyalty. I hope you find what you're looking for."

He released her hand, gave a little bow and walked away to join a petite ashen-haired woman who must be Conner's mother. The woman smiled at her uncertainly, then they both turned and vanished into the crowd.

Okay. That was very weird. Talk about cryptic.

"Who was that old geezer?" Gabe asked.

"Michael Rothchild."

"Dude! You know them, too? Man, Vera, for someone who doesn't get out much, you sure get around."

He had no idea.

She turned to Gabe. It was getting late, and she was ready to call it a night. She'd been dancing around the topic of Darla and her craziness with everyone all night and gotten nowhere. So she decided to just come out and ask. "Gabe, have you ever heard of Darla being involved in anything illegal?"

He regarded her skeptically. "Like what?"

"Like stealing jewelry."

"Whoa, dude." He shook his head. "No, nothing like that."

Vera nodded. "Good. I'd heard a rumor. But I just couldn't believe it myself." She met his eyes. "If you ever hear of her being involved in—"

"What the *hell* are *you* doing here?" The furious words were growled from behind. A firm male hand clamped around her arm and yanked her away from the group, then pushed her off toward a large potted palm that was part of the decor. She could hardly keep up and nearly tripped several times. Alarm zoomed through her. He wouldn't let her turn to look at him. But he didn't have the right color hair. It was thick and silver. Like—

She gasped. *Please, anything but this.*

They were attracting stares, so he slowed down until they reached the palm, then spun her to face him.

God help her. It *was* him.

Maximillian St. Giles.

Her father.

Vera's heart thundered so hard she was afraid it would pound out of her chest. She opened her mouth, but didn't know what to say. "Hello, Daddy," somehow didn't seem appropriate. So she firmly shut it again.

"You little gold-digging whore," he snarled, his piercing green eyes identical to her own glaring at her in hatred. "What do you think you're doing here?"

The *bastard.*

She resisted the urge to slap him across his sanctimonious face. For the insult. For all the insults she'd endured over the past twenty-four years. For snubbing her her entire life. For abandoning her mother, leaving the poor woman pregnant and alone with only a token cash settlement as compensation for a ruined life. But mostly for being a selfish, womanizing, egotistical prick.

She resisted, but her control was hard-won. She started to shake with bitter fury. And a stinging hurt that refused to be ignored.

"Why I'm here is none of your business," she snapped, glaring at his hand on her arm. She'd dealt with plenty of men like him. Bullies covering up their insecurities with threats of violence. "Let me go, or I'll call security."

He finally let her go. And leaned his anger-reddened face right into hers. "It *is* my business if you've come here to make trouble for me and my family."

"Trust me, you are not worth the bother," she spit out, keeping her chin up, shoulders straight. She *wouldn't* let him intimidate her.

"You've been asking questions about my daughter," he accused. "My *real* daughter."

More pain sliced through her chest. How could he *say* that? She fought to keep tears from filling her eyes. She wouldn't give him the satisfaction. "Darla's disappeared. I'm worried about her."

He snorted. "More like upset she's not there for you to leech off."

She curled her hand into a fist to keep from smacking him. But maybe she should give in to her first impulse. A fist in that hypocritical, self-righteous face sounded really good about now.

"Get out of here," her father sneered. "Go back to that strip club where you belong. And if I catch you asking questions about my daughter again, I'll hit you with legal action so hard you'll be living on a grate for the rest of your life."

With that, he turned on a heel and stormed off.

She stood watching his wake disappear into the crowd, fighting to control the trembling in her limbs.

Okay, then.

Another sentimental family reunion. Always a fun time.

"Are you all right?"

She looked up to see Conner. Her tongue tied in knots and she couldn't speak. Because suddenly, she had a blinding insight.

Conner Rothchild was just like her father.

Oh, not abusive, or overtly insulting. Nothing like that. But he was the same kind of man. With the same kind of lifestyle. And the same kind of prejudices. Against people like her.

Conner was *ashamed* of her.

That was why he'd insisted she come to the event as his assistant. Why he'd accepted a date with Ms. *Paris Vogue.* Why he hadn't told his brother, or anyone, the true nature of his relationship with Vera. If you could call two days of monkey sex a relationship.

"N-no," she stammered. Shook her head. "I mean yes. I'm fine. Really. Go back to your date."

"I don't want to—"

"Conner, please. I'm tired. There's nothing more to learn here. I'm going home now."

He frowned, managing to look concerned. Maybe he really did care. Yeah, that she'd blow their cover and reveal herself to his blue-blood family. She'd seen him with his famous hotel magnate uncle, Harold Rothchild, and his young trophy wife. Wouldn't they get a kick out of—

No, stop it. Conner wasn't like that.

Except he was. And now finally both of them knew it.

"I'll call the limo for you," he said.

"No. I'll take a cab."

"Don't be ridiculous." He pulled his cell phone from his tuxedo pocket.

"All right, fine." She didn't want to argue. She just wanted to be gone from this nightmare of a night.

"The driver has the pass code for the gate."

For a second she didn't know what he meant. Then it hit her. He expected her to go back to *his* home.

Can you say no way in hell? But she decided not to tell *him* that. "Yes, I remember."

"Good. I'll tell Hildy to be expecting you."

It occurred to her that this must be a huge relief for him. Now he wouldn't have to come up with lame excuses as to why he needed to drop his assistant off *after* he dropped off his date. She'd just be waiting for him at home. Preferably in bed. Preferably nude.

No wonder he hadn't protested.

She went to take off the ring. "You should take this."

"No, keep it for now," he said.

She couldn't argue or he'd know she had no intention of going to his place. She'd just have to send it back to him tomorrow.

"All right. Go." She made a shooing motion. "Your friends will be wondering where you are."

He hesitated, his brow furrowed. "Are you sure you're okay? You look…"

"I'm fine," she lied. "Go find your lady."

"She's not—"

But Vera was already walking away, not listening. *Back straight, head up,* she told herself as she threaded through the throng. How many of these strangers had witnessed Maximillian's tirade against her? It didn't matter. She just had to make it to the door without being stopped. *Pretend you're on the catwalk. You're not naked,* they *are.*

"Vera?"

Oh, God, now what?

She resolutely ignored the unfamiliar male voice and went right on walking.

Long fingers grasped her shoulder. "Vera, wait."

She suddenly remembered the thief. She opened her mouth to scream. But then she recognized who it was. From pictures. In her living room.

"I'm Henry St. Giles," he said, removing his hand. "Darla's brother."

Fortyish with thinning hair, he was still good-looking in a boring businessman sort of way. Darla was always telling stories about his out-of-control, crazy youth, but somehow he'd ended up selling out to their father and going to work for him after he was cut off for a year. Which explained why they'd never met.

"I know who you are," she said curtly, bracing herself for round two. "What do you want?"

He looked abashed. "I'm sorry, Vera. I just wanted to apologize for what happened back there. With my father."

"Why?" she asked suspiciously.

"We don't all think the way he does."

She arched a brow but didn't comment.

"I know you have no reason to believe me," he continued, "but I honestly regret not getting to know you like Darla did. You're my little sister. I should have made the effort, not cowed under to my father's…stupidity."

Wow. She hadn't known what to expect from Henry St. Giles when he stopped her, but this definitely wasn't even on the list.

"That's, um, very nice of you to say." Not that she particularly believed him.

"You look like her," he said, with a little smile.

"Yeah. So we've been told."

The man actually looked bashful. Either he was a hell of an actor or he was sincere. You could have knocked her over with a feather.

He held out a business card to her. "This is me. I've written my private line on the back. Call me. I'd love to get together for lunch or dinner. Get to know you. If you like."

She decided to be flattered. "Thanks. Maybe I will." Could she actually be getting a brother? She reached for the card. The second he spotted the ring on her finger, Henry's eyes popped. "What the—" They shot to hers in shock, even wider. "Vera, is that what I think it is? The ring from Candace Rothchild's murder?"

She smiled at his bewilderment and shook her head. "No. It's paste. Pretty good copy, though, don't you think?"

"Where on earth did you get it?" he asked, still awestruck by the jewel.

"Long story," she said with a laugh.

"I thought it was stolen?"

"No, the original was stolen. Well, actually both. But now they're back—"

"Miss Mancuso?" the doorman interrupted. "Your limo is here, miss."

"Thanks, I'll be right there." She tucked Henry's card in her beaded bag and held out her hand to him. "It was nice to finally meet you, Henry. And I will call. I look forward to lunch."

He nodded and waited just inside the entrance, watching as she walked to the white stretch limo and got in. He waved as the chauffeur closed the door.

Vera let out a long sigh of relief, bending down to pull off her shoes and wiggle her toes on the plush limo carpet. Thank God the night was over. Just one more thing to do. She picked up the phone to the driver.

"Yes, Miss Mancuso?"

She gave him her home address.

"But Mr. Rothchild said—"

"Change of plans," she said. "Just take me to the address I gave you."

"Very well, Miss Mancuso."

She didn't want to think about Conner right now. Didn't want to let herself be depressed about their doomed affair. Or her bastard of a father. Or even about not making any headway on the investigation of Darla and the theft ring.

She did smile when she thought of Henry. Well, at least the night hadn't been a total disaster.

Her brother. Who'd have thought he'd want to get to know her after all this time?

It was so amazing, it almost made up for losing Conner.

Almost.

Chapter 14

"Babe? Where are you?" Conner jetted out an impatient breath. "Vera, pick up the damn phone!"

Her answering machine clicked on. Conner slammed down his receiver and paced back and forth in frustration. "Damn it!" Where *was* she? She must be there. Ignoring him.

He *knew* he'd be in trouble over that freaking date.

He ripped off his bow tie and threw it onto his bed. The bed Vera should be tucked into, waiting for him.

Not that he blamed her, if he were honest. He wouldn't have been nearly as civilized about it as she was if *she'd* turned up with a date for the evening. He would have ripped the guy's throat out.

Or at least kicked him out of the limo onto his damn ass.

He picked up the phone again and dialed the number of the bodyguard he'd hired to follow her tonight.

"Barton."

"Where is she?" he demanded, not bothering with the niceties.

Barton rattled off the address of her apartment. "Limo dropped her off just over an hour ago. She's still up there."

"You sure? She's not answering her phone."

Barton was wise enough not to comment. "I'm camped out in the lobby, and I paid the security guy to keep an eye on her, too. I'll know if she budges."

"Good. Anything else I should know about tonight?"

"Some guy spoke to her as she was leaving the event." Conner heard the sound of notebook pages being flipped. "Name of Henry St. Giles. Gave her a business card."

Darla's brother? Hell, *Vera's* brother. What did *he* want? "Was it amicable?"

"Seemed to be."

As opposed to her confrontation with Maximillian. Her own father. "You'll be there all night?"

"That's the plan."

"Good. I'll expect your full report in the morning."

"Will do, sir."

Thoughtfully, Conner put the phone back in its stand. Should he go check on her? Or just let her cool off… He wasn't too worried about her safety, not with Barton there standing guard all night. And Conner'd hired a cleaning crew to tidy up the apartment after the FBI was done with their evidence collecting, so she didn't have to deal with that.

But, damn it, he *missed* her.

He'd been bored stiff all night, stuck at that stuffy ball with his stuffy family and the stultifyingly sophisticated Annabella Pruitt, slowly drinking himself numb. Or trying to. Unfortunately, he'd remained distressingly sober the entire time, despite the copious amounts of alcohol that had passed through his system.

Guilt?

Possibly.

Probably.

He wasn't proud of the way he'd treated Vera. In fact, he was downright ashamed. What was wrong with him? Was he such a damn wuss that he couldn't just tell his socially paralyzed father to take a flying leap if he didn't like Conner's choice of women?

Not to mention the whole Maximillian St. Giles thing. Conner should have pounded him into the dance floor like a wooden peg. Or at least shamed him into apologizing to his daughter, admitting he was being an ass.

So, why hadn't he?

Because Conner was an even bigger ass, that's why.

Setting his lips in a thin line, he strode into the hall. "Hildy!" he yelled. "Get the limo back here! I'm going out again."

Naturally, Vera refused to answer the intercom. So Conner had to talk the security guard into letting him into the penthouse.

Luckily, he'd been introduced as Vera's lawyer the other day after the break-in, so he didn't have too much trouble convincing the man he was worried about his client and wanted to check on her well-being. The C-note deposited discreetly in his uniform pocket didn't hurt either.

Conner found her in the bathtub. Up to her neck in bubbles, the mirrors steamed up and a dozen scented candles lit. The room smelled like a hothouse filled with damask roses. A bottle of red wine was propped on the edge of the tub. Half-empty. No glass.

The fake Quetzal was sitting on the tub's front rim, winking in the candlelight like a multicolored disco ball.

"Go away," she mumbled, not opening her eyes.

"How do you know who it is?" he asked, chagrined that she wasn't worried and didn't even check. He could be the thief returning, for all she knew!

"I can smell you," she said thickly. "The demonic scent of wealth and temptation."

Had he just been insulted? He made a mental note to change his cologne.

He stepped into the room and closed the door. "Sweetheart—"

"Don't!" Her hand shot up from the water, fanning out a cascade of droplets. "Don't you 'sweetheart' me, you..."

His eyes widened as she called him a *very* bad name.

Ho-*kay,* then. Looked like he wasn't the only one drinking himself into oblivion. "Been watching reruns of Deadwood?" he muttered. Walking over, he plucked the wine bottle from the tub and deposited it on the marble vanity counter.

"Hey!"

"Any more of that stuff and you'll drown yourself," he said.

"Drown *you,* you mean," she muttered. Then called him that word again.

Okay, so maybe he deserved the moniker. But he couldn't help smiling. She was even more beautiful when she was calling him bad names.

"Vera, I'm sorry."

"Tell it to someone who cares."

"Look, honey, I know you're mad, but—"

"Mad? Me?" She cracked an eyelid, gave him a gimlet eye and made a really rude noise.

"I can see you're not going to make this easy on me."

"Sure, I am. What part of 'go away' don't you get? I'll be happy to e'splain it to you." She hiccupped.

He desperately wanted to chuckle. But he figured it would be the last thing he ever did. So he did the second best thing. Toed off his shoes and socks and climbed into the tub with her. They'd have to cut his tuxedo pants off him, but what the hell, he didn't like this suit anyway.

"What the—" she sputtered, wheeling her arms to get away from him. But he just grabbed onto her and held tight as he slid down behind her into the water, leaning his back against the end of the oversize spa tub. "You are such a freaking Neanderthal," she gritted out.

"So sue me. But I warn you, I'll win."

Damn, it felt weird taking a bath in his clothes. But she really would have screamed bloody murder if he'd gotten undressed.

Besides, he didn't want to give her the wrong idea, either. He wasn't here for sex. He was here for forgiveness. For her.

At least she wasn't fighting him anymore. With a huff, she let herself fall back against his chest, closed her eyes again and refused to look at him.

Progress.

She sighed. "Conner, what are you doing here?" she asked him, sounding suspiciously uninebriated.

"Apologizing."

"That's not what it feels like," she said dryly.

He realized his hand had unconsciously found its way to her breast and was gently fondling it. Since she hadn't clawed his eyes out, he didn't stop.

He kissed the top of her head. "I'm sorry, Vera. I acted like a jackass. You have every reason to be angry with me, and I wouldn't blame you if you never spoke to me again."

"Good, because I don't plan to."

"Which would be a damn shame, because I'd really miss you ordering me around when we're in bed."

Instead of snorting and telling him *he* was the one who did all of the ordering around, as he'd hoped she would, she just sighed again.

"Conner, you and I, we're not going to work," she said quietly. "I don't fit into your world. I'd never be accepted by your family. What's the point?"

He hugged her closer, leaning his cheek on her head. "Because I don't want to give you up."

"You did a pretty damn good imitation of it tonight."

Guilt assailed him anew. "I know. And I couldn't be sorrier. I was wrong. It'll never happen again. I swear."

"You're positive?" she asked bleakly. "Because if it came down to a choice between me or Rothchild, Rothchild and Bennigan, I have a feeling I know which way it would go."

"I'm not so sure." He fell silent, and for the first time he seriously thought about what would happen to him if he left the family law firm. Or was asked to leave.

Would he be sad? Sure, he would. Would it take a while to regroup and start over? Undoubtedly. But he had more than enough money in the bank never to have to work another day in his life. So would his world fall apart? Definitely not.

The only question was, if it came down to a choice between Vera and his *family,* which way would *that* go?

"You're jousting at windmills," she murmured.

She sounded tired. And he was totally beat himself.

"Let's get out of this water," he said. "And go to bed. We can talk about all this in the morning."

"Conner…"

He kissed her on the temple. "We don't have to make love if you don't want to. Just let me hold you while you sleep."

She hesitated, then let out a resigned breath. "You're a real bastard, you know that?"

He'd been upgraded. A good sign. "I'll take it," he said, kissing her ear. "As long as I can be with you tonight."

The next morning Vera got breakfast in bed. It was Saturday, and Conner didn't have to work.

The sun was streaming through the floor-to-ceiling bedroom windows looking out over the city below and the mountains beyond. The sky was so blue it hurt. A lone hawk rode the thermals that rose off the desert floor, scouting for its morning meal…or maybe just windsurfing for the sheer joy of it.

She had no right to be so happy. She knew the bliss wouldn't last. Conner was fooling himself if he thought they had a prayer.

But it was enough that he wanted to try.

Or said he did.

That was a miracle in itself.

He'd made no declarations of love, given her no vows of forever. She could live with that. For now. Just having him here with her was more than she'd ever expected.

"Coffee?"

"Mmm." It smelled delicious. "Who made the French toast?"

"I did," he said proudly.

She was impressed. "A man of many talents."

He leaned over and gave her a slow, thorough kiss. "And a woman of rare appetite," he said in a low rumble.

They'd made love. Of course they had. Like she could take him to her bed and not touch him. Not have him touch her. Impossible.

He'd been so tender it nearly broke her heart. It almost felt like… No, she wasn't going there.

They'd just nestled together into the propped-up pillows to eat the savory breakfast, when his cell phone rang. He checked the screen.

"It's the office. Guess I'd better get it." They rarely called him on weekends, so when they did it was usually important.

"Conner here."

"It's your father."

Hell. "Hi, Dad. What's up?"

"You got an e-mail about a surveillance from someone named Barton."

Conner glanced at Vera and smiled. "Yeah?" How the hell had his father gotten hold of that?

"It came in on the general e-mail account," his dad said, answering the unspoken question. "You're surveilling Vera Mancuso? What's that all about?"

Double hell. "Hang on, Dad." He climbed out of bed, giving Vera a kiss. "Reception's bad in here. I'm gonna take this outside." He grabbed a towel to wrap around his waist and trotted out the double sliders to the huge tiled patio that circled the penthouse, closing them firmly behind him.

"I told you about the case she's helping me on. The whole Quetzal thing. She could be in danger, so I'm making sure she's safe."

"From between her sheets? Mike says—"

Anger shot through Conner. He tamped it down. "That's none of Mike's business, Dad. Or yours."

"It is if I think you're getting personally involved with this woman."

"Why would that matter?"

"You have the family name to think of."

"Oh. You mean like Uncle Harold? Or Candace, or Silver?" All stars of the local gossip columns due to their endless "inappropriate" love affairs. Although Silver seemed to have settled down now that she was a newlywed and expecting a baby.

"That's not our side of the family. *Our* side—"

"I know, I know. We're the respectable ones. We only defend murderers and rapists. But we marry decent women."

His father made a choking noise. "If you have a problem being a defense attorney—"

"I don't. But if I want to date a stripper, I'll date a stripper. Besides, it's not serious." Yet. "I just met the woman. No doubt I'll get tired of her soon, just like I get tired of all the women I date."

It was disturbing how easily the half-lie slipped out. Half, because he *did* go through women like popcorn at the movies. But he didn't want to deal with his father now. He *had* just met Vera, and although his feelings about her were totally different than for any other woman he'd ever dated, how could he be so sure she was The One? That this affair was forever? Why alienate his dad until he was a hundred percent certain?

That wasn't being a coward. That was being prudent.

"Did you at least get the paste Quetzal back from her? That's an extremely valuable piece of jewelry."

"Yes, Dad. I got it back," he said exasperatedly. And made a mental note to retrieve it from the tub.

"All right. Good. Anyway, just be careful, son. Women like her—"

"I will, Dad. Don't worry. Just forward the e-mail to my private account, okay?"

"Your mother is asking if you'll come to dinner tonight. Ms. Pruitt and her father will be here."

Saints preserve him. "Sorry, can't make it. I've got a good lead on the Parker case and will be working it tonight until all hours."

"The Parker case?"

"One of my pro bonos."

"I see. Conner, I really wish—"

"I know, Dad. Give Mom a kiss for me."

He punched the end button on the cell phone with an annoyed curse. He knew his dad meant well. But he was all grown up now—thirty-three years old. He could run his own life.

And if he wanted Vera in it, that was *his* decision to make, no one else's.

Chapter 15

It's not serious... No doubt I'll get tired of her soon...

Vera hadn't meant to eavesdrop. She really hadn't. She'd just gone into the bathroom and noticed it was still humid from last night's bath and opened a window. Could she help it if Conner was talking on the phone practically right under it?

And now his casual pronouncement was seared into her brain.

Nothing she hadn't already known. Nothing she hadn't been telling herself over and over for the past three days.

But hearing it spoken out loud like that, from her lover's own mouth in such a matter-of-fact manner, well, that really brought it home with a sick thud in her heart.

Everything he'd said last night was a lie. She really was just a temporary plaything for him.

As her mother had been for her father.

For the first time ever, she finally understood why her mother had done what she had. Thrown away her life for a man who didn't care about her for more than a few nights of pleasure. She'd been in love with wealthy, powerful Maximillian St. Giles, just as Vera was in love with wealthy, powerful Conner Rothchild. And love made women do foolish, foolish things.

Taking a deep cleansing breath, Vera quickly finished up and slid back into bed before he knew she'd overheard his conversation.

For now it didn't change anything. Outwardly. But she was so glad she'd found out his true feelings. Or she might have believed his pretty lies and allowed herself to dream of the impossible. Heartbreaking as it was, better to know the truth.

Putting on her best smile, she greeted Conner with a kiss when he came back to bed.

"Mmm," he hummed approvingly. "You taste sweet."

"You'll never guess what I found on the breakfast tray."

He grinned against her mouth. "Yeah? What's that?"

She held up a can of whipped cream. "Funny, I don't remember this being in the kitchen yesterday."

"I found it in the limo fridge. Those chauffeurs do think of everything, don't they?"

She squirted a dollop on her finger and slid it into her mouth suggestively. "Gee, and I thought you didn't come here for sex last night."

His grin widened. "A man can always hope, can't he? I did apologize. Abjectly and sincerely. *And* I ruined my tuxedo getting back into your good graces."

"Or pants, as the case may be."

"As I recall, there were no pants involved."

"Hmm." She flipped back the covers, revealing his magnificent naked body. His magnificent and *aroused* naked body. "It appears you're right."

His eyes went half-lidded. "I was talking about you."

"And I," she said, giving the can a shake, and then a well-aimed squirt, "was talking about you."

He moaned as she bent to lick the sweet cream from his shaft, melting back onto the pillows in willing surrender to her tongue.

He may well give her up in the end, but when he did, he'd be giving up the best damn lover he'd ever had. She'd make sure he remembered her for the rest of his life, seeing her face in the face of every future lover, feeling her touch in every brush of their fingertips.

He might give her up. But he'd always regret letting her go.

Almost as much as she did.

Conner was totally wrung out.

Ho. Lee. Batman.

The woman was amazing. Agile. Clever. Mind-blowing. Among other things.

Last night they'd done tender and loving. The night before had been hot and ravenous. This morning had been…well, every one of his fantasies come true.

Yeow.

She'd left him sprawled limply in bed, waving at him from the door with her fingers and a wicked smile, and gone to visit her stepfather, Joe. It was Saturday, her usual day to have lunch with him at the assisted-care facility.

Conner had a feeling she wouldn't be all that hungry. She'd eaten a ton of whipped cream at breakfast.

Oy.

The woman would be the death of him yet.

But what a way to go.

He *really* did not want to do this.

But he had no choice. It was the only way to get the

evidence he needed to exonerate Suzie Parker and put the scumbags who'd abused her away for good.

Conner reluctantly hit the "Pay Now" button on the PayPal invoice he'd received from Lecherous Lou for tonight's private gentlemen's party. He'd much rather be watching Vera dance at the club. And he was still worried about her safety. So much so he'd put Barton back on her tail after letting him get a few hours of sleep. He'd just called in after catching up with her at the assisted care. The guy was good. And thorough. The report he'd e-mailed this morning was detailed as hell, including background sketches on all the people she'd spent more than five minutes with last night at the charity ball. Apparently, Barton liked to while away his hours on stakeout doing research on the Internet from his BlackBerry.

From his notes, Darla's friends seemed to be mostly aging spoiled rich kids who seemed harmless enough, with no huge red flags among the bunch of them. Her brother, Henry, on the other hand… The guy was a real piece of work. His record up until his early thirties read like a Primer for Troubled Young Men. Everything from joyriding without permission, to a dismissed assault charge for beating up a love rival, to a variety of drunk-driving charges. All dismissed as well. His daddy had very deep pockets.

Conner shot off a note to his secretary to give Barton a raise, then reached for the phone to call Vera's cell.

"Where are you?" he asked when she picked up.

"Are you stalking me, by any chance?" She sounded more amused than irritated.

He sat back in his chair and grinned. "Hell, no. Well. Maybe. But in a good way."

"Good," she said. "Then I know I've got you hooked."

"Hook, line and sinker, baby."

She chuckled softly, but he detected a sadness lurking in the tone.

"Something wrong?" he asked. "Your stepdad okay?"

The question elicited a sigh. "No, not really. He's getting worse. It's so depressing to watch."

"I'm so sorry, sweetheart. I know he means a lot to you."

"Yeah." There was a pause. "So what's up? Where are *you?*"

"At the office catching up. And I'd like to point out, you never actually answered where you are."

She laughed gently. "On the way home. I have *got* to get some sleep before work tonight."

"I've got a few hours free," he said suggestively. "I could come over and—"

"Forget it, Batman. I can barely walk as it is. God knows how I'm going to perform tonight."

He gave a bark of laughter. "That bad?"

She made a throaty moan. "That good."

He sat there beaming. You could pull down the blinds and the room would still be fully lit. "Yeah," he said. "For me, too." He made a frustrated noise. "I sure wish you were here so I could kiss you."

"Me, too. Maybe later?"

"Absolutely." Suddenly, he remembered why he'd called. "Listen, about later. I'm going to have to work until pretty late. There's a lead I need to follow on another case, but it'll only happen tonight."

"Oh. I understand," she said, trying to hide her disappointment but failing. God, she made him feel good.

"I've assigned you a bodyguard," he continued. "His name is Barton, and he'll stay with you at the club until I can get there."

"Really? You think that's necessary?"

"I hope it's not, but I won't take any chances."

She hesitated, then, "Okay."

He breathed a sigh of relief. "Thank you for not arguing."

"I can still feel that gun sticking into my back. Something I'd just as soon not experience again."

"Beautiful *and* smart," he said. "Just do what Barton says, okay?"

"Everything?" she teased.

"Ha-ha. Only if you want me in prison for homicide."

"Sweet-talker."

"You have no idea."

He heard a soft puff of breath. "I'll be waiting for you."

"Your place or mine?"

Her voice went low and throaty. "Where would you like me?"

A loaded question, if ever he'd heard one. He matched her tone. "Where haven't I had you yet?"

"You are so bad."

"That's why you love me."

Suddenly there was an awkward pause.

Ah, hell. Why had he said *that?* He covered quickly. "If I don't get to the club before your shift ends, go to my place, okay? I'll be there as soon as I can. Barton will keep me informed with what's up."

"Right," she said. "I'm home now. Gotta run. Bye."

"Be careful, honey."

But she'd already hung up.

He took a deep breath.

Way to go, idiot. Talk about almost stepping in it. He knew she was deliberately keeping her distance from him emotionally. Which was a *good* thing. Because he was, too. This affair between them was too new, too potentially disastrous, for either of them to take it lightly. Dropping the L-bomb like that…already…not good timing on anyone's clock.

Maybe she hadn't noticed.

Uh-huh.

Which was why she'd been in such an all-fired hurry to hang up.

Damn.

Vera lay in bed staring at the ceiling for two solid hours, trying to take a nap.

It was no use.

Thoughts whirled in her head, around and around at the speed of light, keeping her wide awake. Because when Conner had made that joke about her loving him, she'd almost blurted out and told him the truth. That she really did.

Love him.

Thank God she'd had the presence of mind to stop herself. What a joke. Yeah, on her.

She finally gave up and got ready for work instead. May as well go in and pick up an extra set. At least she'd be using her insomnia productively. She needed all the money she could make.

Joe was worse. A lot worse. He'd picked up an infection in his lungs, and if it didn't get better, it could easily turn into pneumonia. His nurse said a lot of Alzheimer's patients died of pneumonia. So he needed a lot of extra medications. Which cost a lot of extra money.

When she got down to the lobby, a man rose to his feet.

"Are you Burton?" she asked. When he nodded and showed her his ID, she suggested they carpool. "Seems silly to take two vehicles when we're going to the same place."

"Good idea. I'll drive," he said, and made a notation on a small spiral pad.

When they arrived at the Diamond Lounge, Lecherous Lou called her into his office right away. Barton insisted on following her and standing guard outside the door.

Seemed a bit obsessive. But it did make her feel safe.

"So," Lecherous Lou said as soon as the door was closed, "you on for tonight?"

She frowned in confusion. "Well, yeah. That's why I came in early."

He smiled, all teeth. "Great! I knew you'd come around eventually." He leered at her. "Nothing like a big spender to open a woman's eyes—and her legs—I always say."

Wait. "What are you talking about?" Obviously not the same thing she was.

"The private party tonight. You are coming, right?"

Disgust straightened her spine. "No. I've told you a million times—"

"That was before your sugar daddy signed up," he said smugly. He lifted a shoulder. "Naturally, I assumed you'd want to reap the full benefit of his generosity, and not let some other girl in on the action. After all, it's only because of your performance in the VIP room he decided to take me up on my offer."

Conner?

Shock hit her square in the gut. "You're talking about Conner Rothchild? He's going to one of your parties?"

Lou dangled a PayPal receipt in her face. "Want to change your mind? I'm telling you, the man's got a thing for you, babe. Play your cards right and your take-home pay for the night will be in the thousands. Guaranteed."

But her mind was still reeling over the fact that Conner was attending a private stripper party. *Her* Conner!

Okay, so apparently not as hers as she'd thought.

He'd lied to her! He'd said he was working tonight!

What else had he lied about?

No doubt I'll get tired of her soon...

Obviously, not about that part.

She'd been right. He *was* just like her father.

"So, you in?"

Fuming, she gave herself a severe reality check. The jerk wanted a private party? Fine. She'd give him a damn private party.

And then she'd give him a big fat piece of her mind. Right before she left him and his lying self high and dry.

For good.

"Sure," she declared, already planning her exit strategy. "Count me in."

Chapter 16

Conner was wearing a wire. Well, technically, not a wire but a tiny video camera and wireless transmitter, a handy gizmo he'd had a techie friend build into an old Rolex watch a few years back. The device beamed sound and video images to a small laptop, which he'd set up back in his room to record everything. The laptop was being monitored by a Metro vice officer recommended to him by his cousin Natalie.

Lou's party was being held in a luxurious multibedroom suite in one of the most exclusive hotels in Vegas. Unbeknownst to upper management, Conner assumed. He'd registered for a room of his own on the floor directly below, where he'd gotten ready, made sure the vice officer was comfortable and well-stocked for the night, then ridden the elevator up to the party suite.

Imagine his surprise when he found Barton standing guard outside the door.

What the—

He scowled. Heading him off, Barton jammed a thumb in the direction of the door. "Sorry, sir. She took my BlackBerry. I didn't want to leave my post to find a phone."

Conner ground his teeth. What the freaking hell? "It's okay. You did the right thing."

He rang the buzzer and waited for a long minute until the door was answered. When it finally opened, his worst fears were realized.

Vera. Wearing red silk lingerie and red satin high heels.

She looked ready to work. Hell, she looked ready to sin.

"Hello, Mr. Rothchild," she said smoothly. "Welcome."

The unforeseen development threw him for a total loop. Hadn't she said she refused to dance at these parties? "What the *hell* are you doing here?" he demanded under his breath.

"I could ask the same," she said pleasantly, crooking her arm around his elbow and drawing him inside. Except her arm was stiff and her smile glued on.

Which was his first clue that she was furious. *Really* furious.

Oh.

Hell.

Lou must have bragged to her that he was coming tonight. And invited her to join the fun. Damn. He should have anticipated that and told her himself.

"I can explain," he said.

"I'm sure you can," she said, piercing him with a look that would wither flowers. "Although I could have sworn you told me you'd be working on a lead tonight. You know, lawyer stuff."

He glanced around the large, opulent room populated with a dozen well-dressed wealthy men and maybe twenty mostly undressed girls—a couple of whom were not looking happy to be here—making sure they weren't being overheard. Behind them, the buzzer sounded and another man was ushered in by a different lady.

"I *am* working on a lead," he whispered, starting to get ticked, himself. After what they'd shared together, she should have a *little* faith.

She stared at him in abject disbelief.

Conner raised his wrist, pretending to check his Rolex. "Smile for the camera," he gritted out under his breath, and pointed the face at her. "Click."

At least she had the grace to look taken aback. "But…I thought—"

"You thought what?" he quietly demanded, leading her to the side of the room. "That I'd go off looking for a good time somewhere else? That I'd betray you like that? That I can't be *trusted?*"

Her suddenly remorseful face said it all. No. She *hadn't* trusted him.

"Great." He raked his fingers through his hair, not knowing whether to be more hurt or angry. "Thanks for the overwhelming vote of confidence."

"I'm sorry," she whispered contritely. "I didn't know. Lou said—"

"And naturally you believed him, not me. Because *he's* so trustworthy."

Definitely hurt.

Her lips turned down unhappily. "I'm sorry, Conner. The men in my life haven't had the best history for being icons of trust."

His heart zinged. Right. How could he forget? Especially after the scene last night with her own father.

With a monumental effort, he pushed back his anger. Given her background, she had every right to be wary, and he had no right to chastise her for it. With a sigh, he put his arms around her and pulled her into an embrace. "No, *I'm* sorry, honey. This is my fault. I should have told you the whole truth. I just thought—"

"You couldn't trust me?"

He gave her a sardonic smile. "No, I thought maybe you'd get jealous and want to be here for me, regardless of personal consequences. You know, so I wouldn't go with another woman."

She stared at him, chagrin clouding over her pretty green eyes. "Touché." Then her gaze darted to the door, where another pair of men had arrived, and back to him. "What lead *are* you following?"

He sent her a warning look. "Whatever it is, I can't do it with you here," he said in a low voice. "You need to leave."

"But I could help."

He set his jaw. "I don't want you involved."

"But—"

"You should go. Now. Unless you want to wind up arrested, or faced with testifying in open court."

She shook her head, eyes wide. "No."

"I didn't think so." He brushed his fingertips down her cheek. "Go home. Wait for me there." He tilted her chin up and gave her a kiss.

"Okay, I—"

"Well, well, well." They looked up at the nasty tone of an all-too-familiar figure standing next to them. "If it isn't the little gold-digging stripper again."

Conner's back went right up.

Maximillian St. Giles. He should have known a reprobate like St. Giles would show up at one of these things.

Vera's father continued his harangue of her, barely taking a breath. "What's the matter? Didn't find a big enough sucker to leech onto at the ball last night?" He puffed up and tried to look down his nose at Conner but was several inches shorter. He only succeeded in showing off his nose hairs. "Rothchild, isn't it? Michael's oldest. I see you've met my bastard daughter. Careful, she'll—"

Conner couldn't take another word. "The only bastard around here is *you*, St. Giles," he growled, easing Vera protectively behind his body. His hands were literally itching to flatten the jackass. "Tell me, if you're so high and mighty, why are *you* here?"

Maximillian glared. "I have every—"

Conner knew he shouldn't draw attention to himself, but he just couldn't stop from saying, "Not getting it at home? Is that it? The wife finally had enough and cut you off?"

"Why you—"

For every syllable Conner uttered, he was getting angrier and angrier. "Maybe you should try being a little less hypocritical, eh? And clean up that mouth of yours around a lady."

"How dare you! She's no lady."

"Vera is your *daughter*," Conner spat out. "Your own flesh and blood! You should be loving her, taking care of her. Not heaping her with your scorn and two-faced disdain. Forcing her into this lifestyle because you refuse to take responsibility for your own actions. You are one damned poor excuse for a man, St. Giles. You're not fit to clean this woman's shoes."

He turned to find Vera covering her mouth with both hands, tears brimming over her eyelashes. She looked up at him with such an expression of misery, Conner's heart broke right in two. "Ah, sweetheart. Forget him. He's not worth your anguish." He pulled her close, turned her away from the jerk.

Another man hurried up to them anxiously. "Mr. St. Giles, are you having a problem with this girl?" The pimp du jour, no doubt. Without waiting for an answer, the pimp discreetly took her arm and urged her toward one of the bedrooms, presumably to get her things. "We can't have any disruptions. I'm afraid I'm going to have to ask you to leave immediately, Ms. LaRue."

"I understand." She glanced back at Conner, tears glistening on her cheeks. "Thank you," she said, her voice cracking, her heart in her eyes.

"Go on and get your things. I'll take you home," Conner said.

"Oh, but—" She shook her head, wiping her tears, and straightened her shoulders. "No. I'll be fine. You stay, Mr. Rothchild. I know you were looking forward to a night of pleasure." She pretended to toss it off and smile carelessly. "Please don't let this spoil your evening."

"Vera, I really—"

"Here." To his shock, she reached out and unclasped his Rolex, then took Pimp Man's wrist and put the watch on him. She gave Conner a meaningful look. "Mr. Black here is in charge of all the night's entertainment. He'll see to it you have everything you could ever wish for, Mr. Rothchild. Isn't that right, Mr. Black?"

The pimp's eyes were glued greedily to the expensive Rolex. Thank God it actually still functioned. "Everything and more," he assured Conner, glancing at a group of girls who were nervously looking on.

Conner knew what Vera was doing. The vice officer downstairs was probably having an orgasm about now. With the audio-video transmitter on the very man who set the price for every criminal act being committed here tonight, they'd have ample ammunition to make the man testify against the club managers who ran the show, and all the evidence needed to shut down these parties for good.

But Conner had never been so torn in his life. He *had* to stay. Make sure nothing went wrong. Set Black up to get the best evidence possible and protect the girls who didn't want to do the things they were being coerced into doing. But if he stayed, Vera would go home alone and crushed. Again. He'd seen how hard she'd taken her father's rejection yesterday. He didn't want to think about the tears she would surely shed tonight if he wasn't there to help her through the emotional turmoil.

"Vera—"

"It's okay, Mr. Rothchild. We'll hook up next time." She went up on her toes and gave him a long, sensual kiss filled with warmth and promise. "And I'll be sure to thank you properly."

He kissed her back, barely able to keep the love and concern spinning around inside him from bursting out of his chest. He whispered, "Promise you'll go to my place."

She nodded and gave him one last hug, then was whisked away by Mr. Black.

A few moments later, head held high, dressed and carrying her purse, she was escorted out of the suite.

He turned to see Maximillian St. Giles watching her with a look of guarded unease on his face.

The bastard.

Conner couldn't help himself. He clamped his jaw, pulled back his fist and punched the man as hard as he could.

Miraculously, Conner's not-so-little outburst did not cost him the Parker case. For some reason, St. Giles didn't press charges. In fact, he was strangely docile about the whole thing. He got up, brushed himself off, excused himself with as few words and as much dignity as he could muster and left the hotel.

After things settled down, for the next several hours Conner walked a tightrope between pretending to be a conscienceless lecher who was interested in the dozen or so women thrust at him by Mr. Black and pretending to drink copious amounts of the champagne they kept filling his glass with. He sure hoped the potted geraniums survived. All the while convincing everyone he really didn't give a damn about Vera other than her body. That Sensitive New-Age Guy performance earlier? Just him trying to get laid.

It would have stretched the thespian skills of a seasoned actor, let alone a lawyer whose skills in that direction came solely from the drama of the courtroom.

Somehow he managed to pull it off, though, and by around three in the morning the officer downstairs had gotten enough evidence to send the Metro vice squad bursting into the suite to take down the whole operation. Everyone got arrested except Conner. But he nevertheless spent the rest of the night arranging bail and deals for the handful of dancers who'd been coerced into working the private party. They'd be good witnesses, and their testimony would corroborate the story of his original client, Suzie Parker, and her prostitution charges would be dismissed.

All in all, a very good night's work, but by the time he got out of there, it was almost noon.

He should be proud, and heading home to a well-deserved night's…well, midday's…sleep. Instead, he was breaking all speed limits to get back home to Vera. He was worried about her and couldn't wait to pull her into his arms and sink down into his bed and just let out a long sigh of relief that she was okay. Maybe get a little sleep before showing her how hard he was falling for her.

Maybe even telling her.

Wow. How terrifying was *that?*

He was just passing the Luxor when his cell phone rang. It was Barton.

"Hey, what's up? Is Vera okay?"

"She's fine, Mr. Rothchild. As I texted you, I drove her to your place last night, and your Miss Hildy took good care of her. Put her to bed, and I sat outside her door the whole night. No suspicious activity at all."

"Excellent."

Barton continued, "But this morning she got a call from

Mr. Henry St. Giles and apparently made plans to go out to lunch with him in a few minutes. I'm sorry, sir, I didn't find out until just now. Do you want me to follow them?"

Hell's bells, Barton must be dead on his feet. Conner definitely was, and he'd actually been able to catch a long catnap in an empty LVMPD conference room while everyone was being processed into the system.

He pushed out a breath. "Where are they going, do you know?" Barton named a small restaurant just off the Strip. "Okay, can you make sure she gets there safely? Then you're done for the day. I'll meet you and take over from there."

"Sure thing, Mr. Rothchild."

He thanked the man for his diligence and made a quick right, heading for the restaurant.

He got to the parking lot before Vera and didn't see Henry waiting. Which gave Conner time to figure out how to handle this. It would be stupid for him just to sit in his car and stake out the place. Aside from which, he might easily fall asleep. Or something could happen to her inside the restaurant.

Because to be honest, Conner was a bit concerned about Henry's motives in courting Vera's favor. His sudden appearance in her life out of nowhere was more than a little suspicious.

Conner was not forgetting his assignment for Special Agent Lex Duncan, to narrow down possible suspects in the interstate jewelry theft ring the FBI was trying to crack—the same ring Duncan highly suspected Henry's sister, Darla, of being part of.

Vera was hoping Darla was innocent, but Conner wasn't so sure she was. What would be more natural than a brother-sister team of high-end thieves?

And if either of them was involved in his cousin Candace's murder, Vera could be in genuine danger meeting with Henry. Conner'd already seen Darla arguing with the man he was convinced stole the Quetzal from the police—likely the same man who later attacked Silver and then Vera, searching for the illusive diamond after he'd failed to hang on to it while he had it. Duncan was waiting for more concrete evidence, but Conner was convinced that man was the link between the ring and Candace's murder.

Would it be such a stretch if Henry somehow had his fingers deep in this mess, too? Even if he didn't, he was Maximillian St. Giles's son and heir. What did he want with Vera after all these years? Nothing good, Conner figured.

Conner decided to let Vera and Henry go into the restaurant after they arrived and got seated; then he'd casually walk in and spot them like his being there was a pure coincidence. Vera would probably twig, but after her quick uptake and play-along last night, he wasn't worried she'd give him away.

That way he could simply join them for lunch. Vera would be safe. And he could subtly pump Henry for information while they ate.

Problem solved.

Except, unfortunately, that's not how things worked out.

Henry arrived first, not unexpectedly. He should have realized something was up when the other man didn't let the valet park his car. But Conner was distracted by Barton cruising past the McLaren and giving Conner a thumbs-up, indicating Vera was right behind him.

Henry, leaning against the door of his Lexus, waved to Vera when she drove into the lot and let the valet whisk her Camry away. Conner raised a brow at the touching hug they exchanged, Henry smiling broadly as he then teasingly touched her earlobe. *Oh, please. Don't fall for it, sweetheart.* The guy had serious bloodsucking scum written all over him. How could Vera possibly miss that transparently fake smarm?

Because she was looking for something else in the man. Like acceptance. Affection. Warmth.

Family.

But still, Conner was not prepared when Henry went around and opened the passenger door for her and she climbed into the Lexus. With a spin of the wheels, Henry peeled out of the parking lot.

Whoa! What had just happened? Had they decided to go to a different restaurant? Or was something else going on?

Conner jackknifed up, gunned the engine and took off after them.

When Henry made a sharp turn onto an all-too-conveniently-situated freeway ramp onto the I-15 south, the major route heading out of the city, Conner really started to worry. So much so that he pulled out his phone and speed-dialed Duncan and then his cousin Natalie.

He wanted backup. Just in case.

Because suddenly, he had a really, really bad feeling about this whole thing.

Chapter 17

"Where are we going, again?" Vera glanced around at the downtown area fast disappearing behind them and bit her lip. "I thought you were taking me to lunch."

"I am!" Henry grinned over at her. "There is this amazing little bistro up in the mountains above Henderson I want you to try. Very chichi. The food there is so incredible, and the view is spectacular. You can see all the way to Lake Mead."

"Okay…" Vera knew Henderson was a growing tourist destination all on its own, but she'd never heard about a fantastic restaurant in the mountains *above* the Vegas suburb. But Henry—she couldn't believe she was finally getting to know her brother!—was presumably a lot more dialed into the hideaways of the rich and famous.

"You're not in a hurry, are you?" he asked politely, even though he was driving like a speed demon.

"No, of course not," she rushed to say. She didn't want to

annoy him the first time they did anything together. Either about his choice of restaurants or his driving habits. She smiled over at him. "I can't wait."

But still… When he bypassed the main exit to Henderson but took a long back road in, she started getting concerned. Not nervous, exactly. More like…uneasy. But he was happily chatting about the Lights of Vegas Charity Ball and how he wished he'd known earlier she was there, and how terribly embarrassed he'd been about his father's—*their* father's, he quickly corrected himself—behavior that night, and how he'd heard so many good things about her from Darla. He seemed so kind and attentive that Vera just couldn't interrogate him about their destination.

Nevertheless, she wished she'd called Conner to tell him where she was going.

Lord, she'd been so upset last night when he never came home. She'd stared at the ceiling until the sun was streaming through the windows and still he hadn't gotten home. In her mind she knew why. She understood what he was doing. That he was not cheating on her. That he hadn't gotten tired of her already and was out having fun with another woman. He was working. He'd probably gotten caught up in…well, God knew what. But whatever it was, she was sure he had a good reason why he couldn't be there for her.

But she'd needed him so badly. She'd been devastated by her father's renewed attack on her and had desperately wanted Conner's warm, comforting presence to soothe the razor-sharp pain in her heart. And in that same hurting heart, she'd felt the slightest bit betrayed.

Even though she knew it was wrong to blame him, that he had an important job to do, she'd been mad enough to arrange this lunch with her brother and take off without paying any heed to Barton's warnings that she shouldn't leave Conner's house. She saw now she'd been acting like a selfish baby.

Surreptitiously, she glanced in the side mirror to see if she could catch a glimpse of Barton following her. But she hadn't seen him since before leaving the restaurant where she'd met Henry. At least she didn't think so. She thought there might have been someone following far behind them, but it wasn't the same color car as Barton had been driving and had since disappeared. Probably wishful thinking on her part. Last night she'd tried to get him to lie down on the sofa, but he'd insisted on sitting up the whole night on a chair outside her door punching buttons on his ubiquitous BlackBerry. No doubt Barton had figured she was safe having lunch with her own brother and had gone home to get some sleep.

So she was on her own here.

Her heartbeat kicked up as Henry turned the car onto an old macadam road heading up into the craggy desert bluffs. "Doesn't this go up to where all those old quarries are located?" she asked.

He glanced at her in surprise. "You know about those?"

"Doesn't everyone?" She gripped the car seat with her fingers. "Are you *sure* this is the way to the bistro?"

"Actually, we're making a quick stop first."

Okay, now she was officially nervous. "Where?" She hadn't been able to stop her voice from squeaking.

He glanced over at her, an enigmatic look on his face. "To see Darla."

"What!?" Confusion coursed through her. Along with a tingling of fear. Why wouldn't he have said that in the first place? *Oh, God.* Had she made a horrible mistake trusting him?

Her pulse doubled. She should bail. Even though the car was climbing up a steep incline and on her side a sheer cliff dropped a hundred feet practically straight down, she should jump out right now. Take her chances on foot—if she survived the fall—while they still weren't too far from civilization and she had a shot at making it back alive.

A shot…

Cold fear surged through her veins. What if he had a gun?

"I had to hide her where no one could find her," he said all-too calmly. "You'll understand when you see her."

Yeah, because she was probably *dead.* The man was a sociopath!

Blind panic had her grabbing the door handle and yanking hard. It didn't budge. *Ohgodohgodohgod.* He had the child safety locks on.

"What are you doing?" he barked, slashing her a glare. "Are you nuts?"

"No, but *you* are if you think I'm just going to sit here and—"

Suddenly, he swung the car behind a huge boulder and pulled to a halt amid a cloud of dust that nearly obscured the silhouette of an ancient mining hut.

"Don't be stupid, Vera," he said, unlocking the doors.

She jerked it open and lunged out, taking off at a run. And immediately tripped in the gravelly sand. Hell! She'd wanted to impress Henry so she'd dressed to the nines, including the pair of exorbitantly expensive high heels she'd borrowed from Darla's closet for the ball. The spike heels pierced the sand like tiny jackhammers, and one of them broke off, hurling her forward into a warm body.

She screamed.

"Vera! Oh, thank God you've come!" wailed Darla, grabbing onto her and giving her a death-grip hug, then pulling away to peer frantically into her eyes. "You've got to help me!" Her voice was filled with desperation.

And her face was covered by knuckle-size cuts and livid purple bruises, her wrist wrapped in a discolored bandage.

"Oh, God, Darla! What has that monster done to you?"

"He beat me up," she wailed, "and I didn't know what to do. I'm so sor—"

Behind her, the car door slammed. Vera didn't wait to hear more of Darla's explanation. She kicked off the ruined shoes, and at the same time as she spun to face Henry, she swooped down and grabbed a fist-size rock from the ground, shoving Darla behind her.

"Vera? No! Wait!" Henry rushed toward them, reaching into his pocket. Going for his gun!

She raised her arm, prepared to fling the rock at his head.

"Vera!" Darla grabbed her wrist. "What are you *doing?!*"

Vera hesitated in confusion. Just as a loud gunshot rang out, cracking the air like thunder.

To her shock, Henry cried out and jerked backward, a cloud of red blossoming around his right shoulder as he fell to the ground.

"Henry!" Darla shrieked. "My God, *Henry!*"

He'd been *shot!*

It hadn't happened often, but there had been one or two shootings at the clubs where she'd worked, so Vera knew enough to hit the dirt. She pulled Darla down with her and immediately started tugging her toward Henry and the car.

"What the hell is going on?" she asked, keeping the panic at bay by a thread as they scurried. "Who's shooting at us?" And from where? The hut?

"It's Thomas! Oh, Vera, I'm so sorry I got you into this! He threatened to kill me if we didn't get you up here! You have to believe me, we didn't want to, but he swore he wouldn't hurt any of us if you only came."

Thomas? Darla's ex-boyfriend, Thomas? "*Me?* Why me?"

Another shot erupted and whined off the boulder just above her.

"The ring!" Darla cried in despair. "He wants the diamond ring! You know, the one I told you to hide for me?"

They sprinted the last few feet. "But I don't have it! The police do!"

"What?" Darla looked at her in horror. *"Noooo!* Now we're dead for sure."

But there was no time to explain. They'd reached Henry. "Grab his feet!" she ordered her sister as she put her arms around her brother's chest to drag him to safety behind the vehicle. As she did, a newspaper clipping fluttered from his fingertips. Not a gun.

"Oh, Henry," she murmured distraughtly. He hadn't wanted to kill her. Some maniac was trying to kill *him!*

Three shots in succession punched through the windshield of the Lexus as she and Darla frantically hauled Henry around to the other side between the car and the boulder.

Correction: someone was trying to kill *all three of them.*

Lord. How had she gotten things so wrong?

Darla was sobbing, and if Vera weren't so terrified, she'd be dissolving into tears herself. But her instinct for self-preservation was too strong. It kicked in big time. One advantage of growing up hard and fast, she thought sardonically.

She pulled off her summer jacket and pressed it to Henry's bleeding shoulder. "Here, hold this here," she told Darla, taking her hand and pushing it firmly onto the cloth. "Harder, or he'll bleed to death."

Darla shuddered out a sob but obeyed. "What are you going to do?"

"Get my cell phone."

Vera reached up from the ground and eased open the Lexus door. Immediately a shot took out the driver's window. Lord, how many shots did that gun have? She tried desperately to remember how many Clint Eastwood counted before he asked the bad guy if he felt lucky…

Okay, that *so* didn't matter. *Focus!*

Sucking down a deep breath, she opened the door wide and snaked onto the car's floor on her belly, snagged her purse from the other side and wiggled out again. Success!

She whipped out the phone and frantically hit speed-dial number one. *Conner.*

"Please answer. Please, please, please," she prayed. "I swear, I'll never doubt you again. Or get mad at you. Or do anything to make you—"

"Ver…? Where the…ll are…?" His anxious voice surged across time and space to yell at her. Well, space anyway. Sort of. Static broke up the words, but she got the drift.

She sobbed with relief. "Thank God. Oh, thank God."

"…alk to me, damn it! I…rd *shots*.…where the h…id he take…ou?"

"We're on a little road up in the mountains behind Henderson!" she said, exchanging a desperate look with Darla when Henry moaned in agony. "Nearly up to those old gravel quarries!"

"…reaking know that! *Where?*"

Two more shots blasted through the noon heat, plinking through the car hood and zinging off the engine block right above them.

She and Darla both let out bloodcurdling screams.

"Vera! V…! Are y…ight?" Conner's voice shouted through the phone.

"Yes! Sorry! We're just so scared!"

"Wh…'s wit…ou?"

"Darla and Henry are with me. Henry's been shot! Oh, Conner, he might die if he doesn't get—"

"Vera, list…me! H…the…rn!"

"What?"

"…orn! Hon…e horn!"

"Horn?" What did he— "Oh!" Suddenly hope blasted through her chest. Was he that close by? "Hang on!" She thrust the phone into Darla's lap and crawled partially into the car again. She reached up and gave the horn a hard blast.

This time the bullet came through the passenger door and thwacked into the driver's seat, not twelve inches from her head. She smacked a hand to her mouth to muffle her terrified scream and hit the horn again two more times, then slammed herself down onto the ground. She met Darla's wild, tear-filled eyes again. A bullet must have severed some wires because the horn continued to blare like a siren. Or was it the car alarm?

"Vera! *Vera!*"

She whipped her gaze to the phone in Darla's lap. But Conner's voice wasn't coming from there. It was coming from—

His car fishtailed around the boulder, blasting its horn and spraying gravel all around it like a machine-gun turret. Conner hung out of the driver's-side window shouting her name.

"Conner!" She jumped up and ran straight for him as he dove from the car, rolled and came up sprinting. Belatedly she realized running to him wasn't the smartest move. He grabbed her and lunged back behind the Lexus.

"Get the hell down!"

But no more bullets came at them. No more shots. As they held their breath, the only sounds to be heard were the distant cry of a hawk, the warm breeze rustling through the creosote bushes and the ticking of Conner's car engine.

"Is he gone?" Darla half sobbed in a pathetic whisper.

"Yeah," Conner finally said after a few more tense moments. "I think he is."

And that's when Vera lost it. Sinking down in his arms, she collapsed in a flood of tears.

Chapter 18

Agent Duncan wheeled up ten minutes after Conner in an unmarked SUV, followed closely by Conner's cousin Natalie, who wailed up in a LVMPD cruiser with lights spinning and sirens blaring. Thank God he'd called them when he did.

By now, Conner'd gotten Vera reassured and Darla's hysterics under control, and the three of them had managed to stop Henry's bleeding and make him comfortable until the ambulance could arrive. He was going in and out of consciousness, but Conner was pretty sure he'd live.

Before the cavalry arrived, Conner had refrained from asking more than two questions, since he knew they'd all just have to go through the story again with Duncan. But his mind burned with theories.

Especially after he found a newspaper clipping on the ground. It was an article about the charity fund-raiser held at Luke Montgomery's Janus Casino several months ago. Next to the column was a photo taken at the event, of Candace showing off the Tears of the Quetzal for the camera. On the night of her murder.

Coincidence?

He didn't think so.

That's what had prompted his two questions. That, along with Darla's badly bruised face.

"Did you beat up your sister?" he asked Henry during one of his lucid moments.

Pain flared in the other man's eyes, though Conner couldn't say if it was physical or mental. "No," Henry rasped. "I'd never hurt Darla."

Darla had gasped softly at the question and nodded at her brother's answer. "He wouldn't," she assured Conner brokenly. "Ever."

Satisfied, Conner accepted that and returned his gaze to Henry. "Did you kill Candace Rothchild?" he asked evenly.

Henry's eyes squeezed closed, and he hacked out a dry laugh. "No. She almost got *me* killed." He opened his eyes. "And my sister." He glanced at Vera apologetically. "And now almost my other sister, too."

Baffled, Conner furrowed his brow. "Candace is dead. How could she possibly be behind the shootings today?"

Okay, so three questions.

But Henry slipped into unconsciousness, his mouth going slack, and didn't answer.

"This wasn't Henry's fault, Conner," Vera said. "He was trying to save Darla's life."

But she didn't have a chance to explain further because just then Duncan and Natalie had gotten there and leaped from their vehicles, weapons drawn and shouting orders to their subordinates to fan out and start searching for the gunman Conner had alerted them to as soon as he'd heard the first shots fired.

"Conner! Are you okay?" His cousin Natalie came running up at full tilt, double-fisted grip on her service revolver, looking like a lean, mean cop on a mission.

Conner rose and swept one arm around her waist and gave her a big hug. "I'm good, Nat. Thanks for coming. I know it's not Metro jurisdiction."

She holstered her weapon and squeezed him back. "Are you kidding? Family's family."

It hadn't always been that way. Natalie was Candace's twin sister and had participated fully in the disparagement of young wrong-side-of-the-family Conner. However, Natalie had matured emotionally faster than her twin; she'd realized their taunting was wrong and hurtful and stopped her part of the torment around the time they graduated high school. Candace never had. But then, by that time, Conner had realized she was an equal-opportunity bitch. Family, foe, friend, stranger: she didn't care who she ripped apart. Anyway, over the past ten years or so, he and Natalie had actually become good friends.

Which was probably why her brows hit her hairline when she noticed that his *other* arm was firmly around Vera and that Vera was clinging to him like a limpet to a ship's hull.

Ah, hell.

He knew damned well that whatever Natalie knew, the whole damn Rothchild clan would soon know…which meant word would get back to his parents in about, oh, ten seconds flat.

He really wasn't prepared for this now.

"Natalie, this is Vera Mancuso. Vera, my cousin Natalie," he said to stave off any immediate pointed inquiries, and left it at that, despite Natalie's crazy eye gyrations, and the fact that he refused to let go of Vera even if it meant he was so freaking busted.

"Nice to meet you, Vera," Natalie said. "Wish these were more pleasant circumstances."

"Thanks, me, too," Vera murmured softly.

"Were you and Ms. St. Giles injured?" Natalie asked.

Vera swallowed and darted a glance at Darla, who was holding Henry's hand as the EMTs loaded him onto a stretcher. "I wasn't. Darla was beaten, but I don't have it exactly straight who did it. Not Henry, though," she said and looked up to Conner for support.

"That's what they both claim," he affirmed. "I believe them on that point. But they're obviously involved in some seriously bad stuff. And…" He dug in his pocket and wordlessly handed Natalie the newspaper clipping.

She froze, absorbed the implications in a nanosecond and motioned to Darla to hold out her wrists. "Sorry," she said, bringing out her handcuffs. "I've gotta do this."

"Whatever," Darla said bleakly.

"Come on. You can say goodbye to your brother before he's taken to the hospital."

"Wait!" Vera said and stepped away from Conner to give her sister a mutually tearful hug.

"Thanks, sis," Darla said, choking up. "He really was going to kill us. You saved our lives."

"No," she denied, wiping her tears. "It was Conner who saved the day. I just beeped the horn."

Nevertheless, Darla said, "You've always been my biggest hero," and kissed Vera's cheek as Natalie, for some reason, smiled at *him,* then led Darla away.

"Beeped the horn, my patoot," Conner said, turning back to Vera, who was suddenly preoccupied with wiping the dust off her ruined skirt. "You're far too humble." That's when he noticed she was barefoot. "And what *is* it with you and shoes?" he asked with a tender smile, and swept her up in his arms just to be able to hold her tight. He was so damn proud of her. "I always seem to be carrying you around. Not that I'm complaining," he added in a low murmur in her ear. "Gives me a chance to cop a feel."

She gifted him with a sweet, watery smile. "You really don't have to carry me. If it embarrasses you, I can—"

"Don't be silly. Why would it embarrass me?" Where had *that* come from? He started walking toward the car, then paused. "Um, listen, I'd like a quick word with Duncan. You want to come with? Or…?"

"Would you mind if I just sat in your car and waited?" she asked, nibbling on her lip. "My knees are still shaking so hard I don't know if they'll hold me up. And to be honest…it makes me cry to see my sister in handcuffs."

"My poor darling." He sneaked a kiss onto her hair, brought her to his car and deposited her gently in the passenger seat. "You just relax. There's a bottle of water behind the seat, if you want it."

She nodded, and he could feel her eyes on him as he made his way over to the ambulance where Natalie was still holding the newspaper clipping with her arms folded over her chest. Duncan was talking to Darla while Henry was loaded into the back of the bus.

Duncan turned to Conner as he came up. "I probably shouldn't tell you this…" His lips quirked in resignation. "But I figure you'll hear it all from Detective Rothchild, here, anyway. Besides, I owe you one…seems you've broken my case wide open for me."

"Always happy to be of service to our friends at the Bureau." He winked at Natalie.

Duncan snorted. "Anyway, Ms. St. Giles has corroborated Ms. Mancuso's statement as to how she came into possession of the stolen Tears of the Quetzal ring and has also absolved her sister of all involvement in any jewelry thefts."

Conner smiled. "Vera will be relieved to hear that. Listen,

would you mind if I asked Darla a question?" The ambulance carrying Henry pulled away, and Duncan turned back to Conner, looking uncertain. "I've already read Ms. St. Giles her rights. She doesn't have to say a word."

"I understand."

"Well. Then it's up to her."

"Ask me," Darla said. "I owe you that much for showing up when you did."

Since she'd been read her rights, he also assumed she'd waived her right to an attorney.

"Okay, your brother said *Candace* nearly killed you both. What did he mean by that?"

A dark shadow passed over her face. "As I've already told Special Agent Duncan…if it weren't for her, we wouldn't be in this mess. My brother and I may have stolen a few pieces of jewelry, but we've never hurt anyone. Jeez. We did it for the thrills, not to get ourselves shot at."

"So how'd that happen?"

She unconsciously worried the bandage on her arm. "This guy, Thomas Smythe, approached us maybe six months ago, wanted to join in our—" she shrugged "—you know, the jewelry thing. He and I hit it off at first and we hooked up for a while. But it turns out he was only using me to get close to Candace."

"Why?" Conner asked. Not that anyone ever needed a reason. Candace had been a force of nature, attracting all sorts of people—weirdos and saints alike. They all wanted to bask in the light of her stardust and notoriety. "What did this Thomas guy want with her?"

"Not her," Darla explained. "Thomas was obsessed with the Tears of the Quetzal. I'm telling you, the guy was bonkers. He talked Henry into trying to steal it." She shrugged again. "Hell, why not? Even cut up into smaller stones, it would bring millions. I'd finally be free to do anything I wanted. With or without the approval of my father."

Aha. So Conner's theory about her had been right.

"Anyway, since I was friends with Candace, my job was to persuade her to sneak it out of her daddy's safe." Darla rolled her eyes. "Talk about obsessive. Her old man is nearly as crazy as Thomas about that ring." Suddenly, she remembered who she was talking to and winced at Natalie. "Sorry. I forgot he's your dad, too."

"No, you're right. He does have a major bug up his nose about that ring. He's convinced it's cursed."

Darla nodded vigorously. "Yeah! So did Thomas. But he's got it in his head the ring will give him some sort of special powers. Something about revenge or some nonsense like that. He was never real coherent when he talked about that stuff." Her mouth turned downward. "I should have listened to my instincts. After a while I broke up with the nutcase and stopped baiting Candace to borrow the ring, but Henry still had this deal with him to fence the diamond if he stole it from her."

"So what went wrong?" Conner asked.

She covered her mouth with a trembling hand, then slid it down to unconsciously touch the bruises on her throat. "The night of that big charity deal at Luke Montgomery's casino, it was all over the local news. You know—" she made quote marks with her fingers "—'Film at six! Live from the red carpet!' God, and there she was, wearing the damn thing on national TV! I mean, we knew Thomas would go for it that night."

"Did he?" Duncan asked grimly.

Tears welled in Darla's eyes. "I honestly don't know. When we heard Candace had been murdered and the ring was missing…" She swallowed.

Natalie burst out accusingly, "My God, Darla! He killed her and you didn't come forward? She was your friend!"

"I would have, honest, but Thomas swore he didn't do it!" Darla wailed. "He was furious, and he didn't have the ring, so I believed him!"

That fit, unfortunately. The ring had disappeared after the murder, but then was found in the possession of Luke Montgomery's fiancée, Amanda, hidden in her purse unbeknownst to anyone. There was rampant speculation as to how it had gotten there, but as soon as it was found, Amanda Patterson had turned it over to the police. She hadn't even been in Las Vegas at the time of Candace's murder, so she was never a suspect.

"After the ring turned up in that woman's purse," Darla continued, "the papers all said the police were holding it as evidence. So Thomas hatched this crazy plan to disguise himself as a cop and walk right in there and check it out of the evidence room! And damned if it didn't work!" She sounded amazed.

Conner could see Natalie gritting her teeth. He knew heads had rolled over *that* one. He'd personally seen to it.

"So," Conner asked Darla, "why were you arguing with him outside the cop shop after he pulled it off?"

Her jaw dropped. "How did you know about that?"

"I saw you. I was on my way in."

"So *you're* the one who figured out so quickly he'd left the paste ring in its place!"

Conner nodded. "I recognized the copy. How did he get hold of it, anyway?"

"He claims he posed as a reporter to gain admittance into Harold Rothchild's mansion. Candace had once told him her stepmother kept an old paste copy of the Tears of the Quetzal in her jewelry case in the bedroom upstairs."

Naturally.

Harold's fourth wife was of the trophy variety and not the brightest bulb on the Christmas tree. It was hard to imagine a rational person keeping a million-dollar jewel in a box on the vanity. Oy. She probably thought just because it wasn't the original it wasn't valuable.

"Pretty clever of him," Conner conceded. "Might have worked, too, if Harold hadn't insisted I go and try to get the ring out of police custody."

"Dad never did trust cops," Natalie muttered. An understatement. Harold had not been happy when she became one.

"Apparently not just cops," Darla said. "Candace told us your father refuses to let anyone near the Tears of the Quetzal, ever."

"Yes, but it isn't about trust, it's about that stupid curse," Natalie said with a hint of annoyance.

"Anyway…" Darla cast her eyes downward again, looking honestly distressed. "If I thought for a minute he'd killed Candace, I would have called you, even though it meant getting heat on the jewelry thing. But he swore he didn't touch her." Her eyes welled. "But now, after he did this to me—" she looked up, gestured to her battered face, and her voice grew thready "—and trying to shoot us today…" Her tears spilled over her lashes.

"You think it was him doing the shooting?" Duncan asked.

"I *know* it was. Who else would it be? The man is a damn lunatic. He's *dangerous*. I'll sign a sworn statement, whatever you need to arrest this guy, but I want protection for Henry and me in exchange, until he's behind bars."

"I'll see what I can do to get you a deal," Duncan said. "Rothchild, you coming down to Metro? LVMPD is taking the suspects into custody for now. But I'll need your statement, along with Ms. Mancuso's."

"Sure thing." Hell, Conner'd gone *this* long without sleep, what was another few hours? He was on about his third…or maybe fourth wind, by now. "We'll meet you there."

Natalie waved to him as she led off her prisoner, then

darted a glance over to his car. "By the way, will we see you at dinner tomorrow, Conner?" she called.

"Not sure. I'll let you know," he called back, heading to the driver's-side door.

Lately he'd gotten into the habit of having dinner at the "other" Rothchilds' on Monday nights. But frankly, he'd rather spend the time with Vera. He slid into the car and smiled across at her, but…she was fast asleep. He leaned over and quietly snapped her belt over her lap, planting a kiss on her temple as he did so.

"Conner?" she murmured sleepily, her eyes still closed.

"Yeah, babe."

"You're not my Prince Charming anymore."

He raised his brows in amusement. Was she talking in her sleep? "No?"

"Nmn-mmnh. That was just for one night." She sighed dreamily. "Now you're my knight in shining armor."

He'd take it. "Okay."

"Know who that makes me?"

"No. Who?"

She giggled softly, still not opening her eyes. "Sleeping Beauty." She sighed and snuggled down into the soft leather of the bucket seat. Totally oblivious.

He laughed, marveling at the ability of this amazing woman to take a horrible situation and pluck the one positive note from its depths. Even in her sleep she was relentlessly optimistic and charmingly romantic.

God, he loved her.

Now if he could just get his family to love her the same way…to see all the good in her…to accept her as worthy of the Rothchild name.

Was that too much to ask?

Unfortunately, he feared it just might be.

Chapter 19

Vera was too wiped out to protest when Conner carried her up from his car to her penthouse.

"We've got to stop meeting like this," she murmured.

"Why?" he asked with a grin.

She couldn't think of a damn reason. So she reached up and kissed him. He winked back at her and carried her into the apartment. They were just here for a quick stop on the way to the police station. For shoes. And a change of clothes. The ones she had on were covered in dirt and blood.

"Maybe a quick shower, too?" she asked.

"Only if I can watch."

She smiled demurely. "Or you could join me."

"How quick are we talking here?"

"That all depends."

"On?"

"How good you are at lathering up."

He made a very male sound deep in his throat. "Oh, honey, I'm *real* good."

"I somehow knew that," she said, wrapping her arms around his neck and kissing him all the way to the bathroom.

He set her down and closed the door behind them with a firm click. Then advanced on her, murmuring, "Baby, prepare to be thoroughly lathered."

Conner's cousin Natalie, the homicide detective, only blinked once when he and Vera walked into Metro headquarters still damp from their not-quite-so-quick shower. She did, however, raise an eyebrow in salute to Vera.

Good thing *Conner* wasn't a detective, because he was totally clueless to the whole female-to-female exchange.

Vera was feeling so good, she couldn't help but smile back at the woman. She hoped there wouldn't be fallout because of Natalie's astute observation. She knew Conner's rich family would not be pleased he was dating someone like her. Her own father's ubiquitous "gold-digger" insults rang a constant reminder in her head of how people like the Rothchilds thought of people in her social class. As in poor. Dirt poor.

Whatever. She still had him for today, and that's all that mattered. What tomorrow brought, she'd deal with tomorrow.

Special Agent Duncan was there, too, and took Conner into a conference room to get his statement. Natalie led Vera over to her desk to take hers.

"Sorry about the luxurious accommodations," she quipped, snagging them each a cup of coffee along the way. "Interrogation rooms are all full. Sugar?"

"Just cream," Vera said. "Thanks. No problem."

Natalie very professionally went through the statement procedure, making sure she wrote everything down just right.

Then she handed the papers off to a junior officer to get them typed up for signature.

"So," she began, leaning back in her creaky office chair while they waited, "you and Conner, eh?"

"Um." Ho-boy. She should have known this was coming. Now what? "It's not serious," Vera echoed his words from yesterday morning to his dad, as much as she wished she dared say otherwise. "We just met, really."

Natalie nodded. "I figured as much. Since you weren't at the Lights of Las Vegas Charity Ball with him."

"Oh, I was there," she said without thinking. *Oops.* "Um. Just not *with* him."

Natalie stared at him. "So, you, like, met him there? Or earlier today?" She blinked again. "Please tell me not at the crime scene." She could tell the woman wanted to be scandalized but was only succeeding in being greatly amused. And trying valiantly to hide it.

"Not at the crime scene," Vera confirmed with a half smile. "Actually it was…four days ago." Had it been such a short time? It seemed like she'd known him a lifetime already. And yet…for only hours.

"Yeah? Where'd you meet?"

Vera felt like she was being interrogated.

Oh, wait. She *was* being interrogated. By a homicide detective concerning her favorite cousin. Territory didn't get much more dangerous than that.

Better play this straight, not only because Natalie would see right through lies, but…she may as well know the truth so she wouldn't get all excited about cuz's new girlfriend and blab to the family. Maybe this way she'd keep it to herself, and Conner wouldn't be embarrassed.

"He saw me dance," Vera said. She went to take a sip of

coffee. Except her hand was inexplicably shaking, so hot liquid sloshed over the rim. She hurriedly put it down again.

Natalie opened her top desk drawer and tossed her a napkin. "Can't take me anywhere, either," she said with a commiserating grin. Still trying to be friends. Vera wanted to cry. "So you're a showgirl. Cool. What show do you work?"

Oh. Crap.

She gave up, and looked Conner's cousin in the eyes. "The Diamond Lounge."

"Oh." Then it really registered. "Oh!" Natalie's eyes got wide. "You mean… A *dancer*. That's, um. Nice."

Yeah.

Thank God, the junior officer returned with her statement. She took as little time as possible to read and sign the thing, then rose and held out her hand. "Good to meet you, Detective. I should be going now. Got to get ready for work."

"Oh. Of course. Sure." She shook her hand, mumbled a thanks for the statement and escorted her back to the waiting area out front. "But you do know we shut down the Diamond Lounge last night, right?" she said as Vera was about to leave.

Vera halted. Frowned. "Closed down?"

Natalie said, "Yeah, Conner orchestrated this big sting of club managers over some call-girl deal, and the clubs all shut down until owners can get other management in place. It'll probably be a few days before the club reopens."

"Oh. I had no idea."

"Not surprising. Been a bit busy today," Natalie said wryly.

"Yeah. Well. Thanks for the heads-up. Guess I'll have the night off."

"Oh, and Vera?"

She paused. "Yes?"

"Conner's coming over to our house for dinner on Monday.

Kind of a new tradition, since…" She cleared her throat. "Anyway, we'd love for you to join us, too, if you can make it."

Disbelief sifted through her. Surely, she was kidding.

Just then, the desk sergeant called over to her, "Ms. Mancuso?"

She tore her gaze from Natalie. "Yes?"

"Can you wait for just a moment? There's someone who wants to speak with you before you go."

Rats. Conner must be finished, too. She wasn't sure she could handle being scrutinized next to him, not now that his cousin knew who she really was. Especially not after that unexpected invitation. *He'd* have to field that one. Vera dare not touch it with a ten-foot pole.

But it wasn't Conner who wanted to talk.

The door opened and out walked the last person on earth she wanted to see.

Her father.

No. No, no, *no*. Not here. Not right now.

She spun on a toe and practically sprinted for the door.

"Vera! Wait!" His voice boomed across the reception area.

She fought to hold back sudden tears. Of all days. Why did he *always* have to—

She fumbled with the door handle, unable to get it open. He reached her and put a hand on her shoulder. She stiffened, waiting for the verbal abuse to start.

"Vera. Please. I know I don't deserve it. But for the love of God, please let me say something to you."

He didn't deserve it? More like *she* didn't. Mutely, she took a cleansing breath and turned to face the barrage.

She was shocked at what she saw. His face was gray, haggard, his eyes bloodshot and rimmed with red. One of them was bruised by a half moon of purple.

He swallowed, his Adam's apple bobbing several times. "I just want to say…thank you," he said, shocking her even more.

Was this some kind of cruel trick? She felt her lips part but for the life of her couldn't think of what to say. It was like she'd landed in some kind of weird parallel universe. Dinner invitations from detectives. Thank-you's from her father. What next?

"Darla told me what you did," he choked out. "That you saved her life. And my son's. That they would both be dead now if it weren't for your calm thinking and unselfish bravery."

"She e-exaggerates," Vera stammered. Still waiting for the other shoe to drop.

"Somehow, I don't think so," he said, voice cracking. "I've been wrong about you, Vera. Your whole life, I've treated you like trash because of my own cowardly refusal to confront my feelings about—" He halted. Cleared his throat. "In any case…words can't express how truly sorry I am."

Wow.

Her throat tightened, almost squeezing the air from her windpipe and sending a flood of emotions cascading from her heart. Almost. But she would *not* let herself break down.

Nor would she fling herself into his arms and cry, "Daddy!"

Or even succumb to the shameful temptation of being as mean to him as he'd earned through his own despicable behavior over the years.

"Okay," she managed, thoroughly shell-shocked.

He looked at her desperately. "Please," he begged softly. "Forgive me?"

Tears stung the back of her eyelids, screaming to come out. This was so damn unfair. How could she forgive him after he'd caused her a lifetime of misery? *And* her mother?

How could she not?

"Sure," she rasped out. "I'll forgive you." Someday. "I've got to go now."

She turned, grabbed the entry door handle to escape, then turned back to Natalie, who'd been watching the entire exchange silently, with a studiously neutral look on her face. "Detective Rothchild," Vera said, her voice barely working. "About that dinner tomorrow? I think I'll have to send my regrets. But thanks."

Then she stumbled out the door, gasping down deep, stinging lungfuls of hot desert air as it surrounded her body.

My God. Her whole life she'd been waiting for this very moment. And now that it had come and gone, all she wanted to do was throw up.

She thought briefly of Conner. Oh, how she wanted his arms around her! But this was one thing she had to process on her own, without his nurturing cocoon of emotional protection.

She just needed to think.

"Ms. Mancuso?" A black-haired LVMPD officer waved and approached her.

Oh, God. *No more.* Please!

He smiled genially. "Ms. Mancuso, Detective Rothchild sent me out to give you a ride home. She said you don't have your car with you. Right?"

"Oh. That was thoughtful." Vera almost sagged with relief. Now she wouldn't have to stand here and flag down a taxi.

The officer led the way to a gray sedan parked on the street. "Sorry about the unmarked car. All the cruisers are out."

"It's okay. I'd just as soon not get dropped off at my building by a police car with lights flashing anyway," she said, making a stab at a normal conversation while her insides were still shaking and churning.

He chuckled and opened the passenger door for her, his strong cologne making her nose twitch. "I hear you."

She got in. But instead of going around to the other side,

he said, "I'm afraid I'm going to have to ask you to slide over and drive, Ms. Mancuso."

Her mind went blank. "What? Why?"

He drew his service revolver from its holster and pointed it at her head. "Because if you don't, I'll kill you."

Chapter 20

"Where's Vera?" Conner asked Natalie. He'd expected to see his lover chatting amiably with his cousin, waiting for Duncan and him to wind up their business. Of everyone in his family, he trusted Natalie not to prejudge a person based on her job, so he'd felt comfortable leaving Vera in her charge.

"She left a good while ago," Natalie said, sitting back in her squeaky chair to regard him.

"Oh. Okay." Disappointed, he poured himself another cup of coffee. It was his… Hell, he had no idea, he'd downed so many cups. He was wired, but at least he was awake. Duncan had kept him longer than anticipated…but he thought she'd wait for him anyway.

"There was an incident," Natalie reported.

Conner stopped mid-sip and held his cup still. *Ah, hell.* "Let me guess. Her father." He'd seen Maximillian gliding past the conference-room window, and hoped the bastard wouldn't run into Vera. Apparently hoped in vain.

"How'd you know?"

"The man is an ass. He should be tarred and feathered."

Natalie peered at him over her coffee cup. "The incident was not in the usual vein, from what I gathered."

Worse? Jeez. "Remind me again why I can't just shoot the jerk?" Conner asked her.

"Unspeakable acts in prison," she said without missing a beat. Then cocked her head. "Though, as a notorious defense attorney with close connections to the underworld, you might be spared the worst humiliations. Except by the guards, of course."

He chortled. "Okay, I get the drift. I'll be good. So. What was so unusual about the incident?"

"He apologized to her. Said she'd saved important lives, exhibited 'calm thinking and unselfish bravery,' I think were his exact words."

"*Seriously?* Max St. Giles?"

"Said he'd misjudged her."

"Wow. That's huge."

"So," Natalie said, eyeing him.

"Spit it out," he said.

"A *stripper?*"

"Please. Exotic dancer."

"Conner. Have you *lost* your mind?" she asked, lifting her cup to her lips.

"Possibly," he answered just as evenly. "Nat, I love her."

She sprayed coffee all over her desk.

He opened her top drawer and tossed her a couple of napkins. "What do I do?"

Her gaze said it all. Total, paralyzing astonishment. "Well…"

Just then her phone rang. Saved by the bell.

She grabbed it, bobbled it, recovered. "Rothchild." After a second, her eyes seemed to focus sharply. She stopped breathing—never a good sign. Her gaze sliced to him. "One moment." She handed him the receiver. "It's for you."

As soon as he took it, she jumped up and started making frantic hand movements at the officers across the room. What the—

Suddenly, his heart stalled.

"This is Conner," he barked into the receiver.

"I have something you want, *Conner*," the male voice sneered. "And you have something I want. Trade?"

Conner's blood chilled. "What do—"

There was a muffled sound, and Vera's desperate voice came on. "Conner? Oh, my God, Conner, it's him, it's—"

"Do we have a deal?"

"What is it you want?" Conner forced himself to calmly ask while his pulse pounded through his body like a kettledrum. Natalie was still moving like a blur, listening in while organizing a trace, he assumed.

"The Tears of the Quetzal," he spat out. "You're at the police station, and I know they have it," he said. He, being Thomas Smythe. It had to be him.

The man's next words confirmed it. "One hour. Bring it to the same place you were this morning. Alone. No games. Or your little stripper dies." Then he hung up.

Conner let loose a string of violent curses.

Natalie, being the ever-practical one, swiped up the phone and punched in buttons like it was on fire. "Duncan!" she said. "Get out here. We have a situation."

"This isn't going to work."

Conner loosened his death grip on the steering wheel of the McLaren and flexed his fingers, taking another hairpin turn up the gravel road to the quarry where the shoot-out had taken place earlier.

"It'll work," came the muffled reply from the trunk, where Duncan was curled into a Kevlar ball, probably roasting in there like a pig at a luau. "It has to."

Tell him about it. He'd kill himself if anything happened to Vera because of this stupid, obnoxious ring.

Maybe Uncle Harold was right. Maybe it *was* cursed.

"Sure you can open the trunk from inside?" Conner asked for the dozenth time.

"Got the safety latch in my hand and my gun in the other, just in case."

"Okay." Conner took a deep breath. "Okay."

"Sitrep?" Duncan prodded.

"Almost there," Conner reported. "Just around the bend." He scanned the road and cliffs around him. "Don't see him yet."

"Vera?"

"No sign." All sorts of awful images flowed through Conner's head as he searched the mountain for any sign of anything.

He slowed to maneuver around the giant boulder, pulled up in front of the old mining hut and cut the engine. After the bustle, whistles and constant ka-ching of every venue in Vegas, the lonely mountaintop was disturbingly silent. Had it been this preternaturally quiet this morning?

He got out of the car. A dust devil twirled past. Nothing else moved.

"Smythe!" he shouted. "Thomas Smythe! I have the ring. Let Vera go!"

"Oh, I'll let her go, all right," came the maniacal reply.

Conner whirled toward the voice. Looked up. And his legs almost gave out from under him. "Vera!" he cried.

He could just make her out, dangling over the side of the cliff a hundred feet above them by a rope tied around her wrists. The rope had been threaded through the arm of an old, rickety piece of quarry equipment, a pulley-type affair on the top of the cliff, from which the rope pulled taut down the cliff to the front of the old hut, ending up winding around an old-fashioned hand crank and shaft. A black-haired Hispanic-looking man was holding on to the handle of the crank. For a split second Conner was confused. The man was dressed as a cop.

Then it hit him. Hell. How stupid could he get? Smythe had done it once and gotten away with it. Why not twice?

Sure enough, it was the same man he'd seen arguing with Darla in front of LVMPD. And who had attacked Vera on the street.

The bastard Thomas Smythe. Or whatever the hell his real name was. Duncan had run a check and found no one matching his description with that name. Figured.

In a flash, Conner saw that if Smythe let go of the rusty crank handle the rope would spin off like greased lightning and Vera would plunge down the cliff. To certain death.

Conner was rigid with fear. "Don't do anything rash, Smythe," he said as calmly as he could manage. "I told you I have the ring."

"Show it to me!"

Moving slowly away from his car, Conner reached carefully into his pocket and brought out the jewel. He held it up for the other man to see. Even in the dimming light of the setting sun, the stone glittered and shone, flashing green and blue and purple like a sparkler on the Fourth of July. Almost like the real thing.

For several seconds, Smythe seemed hypnotized by the sight, his eyes blinded with lust and greed, a look of ecstasy coming over his whole face. Conner took the opportunity to move closer. He had to get to that crankshaft before the deranged man let it go. Which Conner was absolutely certain he would do. Darla was right. He was already over the edge.

Conner cringed. Bad analogy. Really bad.

"Hand it over!" the man yelled, letting the crank unwind a whole revolution.

Vera screamed as she plunged several feet down the cliff.

Smythe's muscles strained to stop the movement. "Now! Or I let her go all the way!"

"All right, all right!" Conner said, taking a few steps closer. Close enough to see the gun tucked in the waistband of the man's jeans, the whites of his crazy-wild eyes, the beads of sweat drenching his face…and the deadly intent in his glazed expression as he started to let the handle go for good.

"Nooo!" Conner shouted, and threw the ring in a high arc over Smythe's head at the same time he made a flying leap for the crank's handle, just as it left the other man's hands.

He grabbed it. It whacked him in the chin going around, knocking him silly.

Vera screamed in terror.

He lunged for it again. This time it dug into his stomach, but he managed to hang on. Vera was still screaming and thrashing, making the rope pull all the harder on the handle. Conner could feel it slipping in his sweaty hands.

"Duncan!" he yelled in desperation. The plan had been for the FBI agent to chase Smythe down, shoot him or at least be able to tell the herd of Metro officers waiting below which direction he'd fled in. That wasn't going to happen. "I need your help!" he shouted.

In a flash, the agent was there, helping to hang on to the crank. Between the two of them they got it under control, then let the rope play out slowly to let Vera down without scraping her up too badly.

"Sorry," Conner grunted as they let out the rope. "I'm sorry I couldn't handle this myself. Now you've lost him again."

"Forget it. Vera's life is all that matters," Duncan said grimly. "Don't you worry. We'll get the bastard. And won't he be surprised when he realizes the ring he has is the fake."

They lowered Vera nearly to the ground, and at the last minute, Conner grabbed her. He hugged her fiercely to him, tears blurring his vision as she clung to him and let out a hiccoughed sob. She was shaking like a leaf.

Hell, so was he.

"You're okay now, you're okay now," he told her over and over, as much to convince himself as her.

She was so damn brave.

And at that moment he realized. It didn't matter what his family thought. Or the risk to his career. Or his social position.

Nothing else mattered.

She was his. And he would never, ever let her go.

Chapter 21

Conner didn't think he'd ever be alone again with Vera.

But after waiting an endless amount of time for the trackers to find Thomas Smythe—and failing—Lex Duncan decided they may as well go home for now.

Thank God.

Vera was on the verge of emotional collapse, and Conner hadn't had a wink of sleep in close to forty-eight hours, putting him near the limit of his endurance both physically and mentally. Lex seemed to recognize that.

"I'll take you two home," Natalie told him, looking more than exhausted herself after tramping up and down the steep mountains for hours. "Wouldn't want any more fake-cop incidents."

Vera glanced at her wide-eyed, and Conner managed a weary laugh, appreciating his cousin's stab at black humor.

"Thanks, Nat," he said, and turned over the McLaren's keys to an awestruck young officer. "Scratch it and you'll be washing my cars for the rest of your life," he warned the kid with mock seriousness. Okay, not so mock. Conner loved his car.

Almost as much as he loved the way Vera looked at him when he climbed into the back of Natalie's cruiser with her instead of getting in the front seat.

He just prayed they'd make it back to his place before he passed out. They did. Just barely.

"We'll be expecting you for dinner tomorrow night," Natalie said as a parting shot when they stumbled out onto his driveway. "*Both* of you."

"Nat—"

"Don't argue with me, boy," she said gruffly. "I have a gun, and I know how to use it."

He gave her a halfhearted grin and a tired wave, and she drove away. Ah, well. He could always cancel tomorrow.

He put his arm around Vera. "I'm about to fall over. How 'bout you?"

"I want to spend a week in bed."

And he had a feeling she meant actually to sleep. He'd probably be of a different opinion tomorrow, but right now that sounded like paradise. They went straight to his bedroom, shedding clothes along the way. Five minutes later they were in bed, snuggled up together like puppies in a basket.

Small tremors still sifted through her. He wrapped his body around her in a sheltering, protective shield. So she'd know without a doubt that, if anyone wanted to get to her, they'd have to go through him first.

She sighed, and finally her tense muscles began to relax. Skin to skin, warm and smooth, primal and visceral, he soaked in the feel of her, the smell of her, the sound of her soft, even breathing. And recognized on a soul-deep level that this was

something special. Something once-in-a-lifetime. He kissed
her brow, and she nestled closer. She put her lips to the curve
of his neck, and whispered, "I love you, Conner Rothchild."

He looked down at the woman in his arms, his heart filling
with an unexpected burst of joy and longing, and he wondered
if she was talking in her sleep again. But then she opened her
eyes and smiled up at him.

"Yeah?" he said.

"Yeah," she said.

"I'm glad," he said, and held her close. "So very glad, Vera
Mancuso. Because I love you, too."

"We are well and truly screwed," Conner said, flopping
back in the McLaren's bucket seat.

"Well," Vera mused, "not the most romantic way of putting
it, but I suppose you could say that."

She thought back over the relaxing day. Without a doubt
the happiest day of her life to date. They'd slept over twelve
hours the night before, then slowly awoken to take advantage
of their renewed energy, the glorious weather streaming in
through the windows and the fact that Hildy did not put a
single phone call through to his suite.

Well, until that last one. The *summons,* coming around
midafternoon. Apparently *nobody* told Harold Rothchild he
couldn't speak with his nephew. Whereupon he had told Conner
in no uncertain terms he was to gather his "young lady" and
bring her to dinner that night. Seven o'clock promptly.

They'd gotten ready and left at five o'clock. Conner had
said he wanted to make a stop on the way. Something to give
him the courage he needed to face his family with her on his
arm. She hoped it had worked for him. *She* felt wonderful.

Vera followed Conner's gaze now as he surveyed the Rothchild driveway, brimming with Jaguars, Mercedes, Porsches

and even a Lamborghini. "Looks like they've invited a few people over," he said nervously.

Poor Conner. He wasn't used to being the object of gossip or disapproval. "We can still leave," she told him. "Do this another time."

He glanced at her, pretending not to be scared. He was so sweet it made her heart ache with love. "Hell, no," he said. "If Uncle Harold wants to meet my young lady he's going to damn well meet my young lady." His mouth tilted up. Half of it, anyway.

She was still getting used to the thought of being Conner's anything, let alone romantically linked to him. *His young lady.* She glanced down at her hands. It had a certain ring to it.

He'd said he loved her. More than once. And as unreal as it felt, she believed him. Oh, how she believed him.

But inside, her heart was doing the quickstep. She had to say it. "What if they don't approve of me? What if they tell you you can't—"

"They won't." He cut her off. "And even if they did, I wouldn't care. I don't need their approval."

"But you want it."

He gazed at her. And nodded. "I want them to love you as much as I do. I have to believe they will."

Her heart swelled. "Okay, then let's go find out."

"Right."

He drove up to the house and left the car in the care of a young man who, a hundred years ago, would have been called a stable hand. She wondered vaguely what they called them nowadays…since they took care of cars, not horses.

God. She was mentally babbling again. It happened whenever she was nervous. She really had to quit wandering off into left field or she'd end up like Joe.

At the thought of her stepfather, a rush of warmth filled her. And wonder. The care facility had called her today, informing her that an anonymous donor had set up a fund to pay Joe's bills there for the rest of his life. She'd been shocked. And immediately assumed it was Conner, all set to hang up and tell him thanks but no thanks. But the director had told her in confidence the secret benefactor had been Maximillian St. Giles. After debating with herself all day, she was inclined to accept his generosity. After all, he owed Joe for taking over his role in her life for the past twenty-four years. This was small payment in recompense, but perhaps it would assuage his guilt just a tad. She could give him that much. Forgiveness would take longer, but this was a place to start at least.

"Ready?" Conner asked her.

She squared her shoulders and nodded. "If you are."

"Oh, I'm ready," he murmured, pulling her close to his side, leaning over and putting his lips to hers. He smiled down at her, and her heart did a perfect swan dive into the warm oases of his eyes.

And somehow she knew it would all be okay.

They walked into the Rothchild mansion arm in arm and were immediately surrounded by all of Conner's various cousins. Even his brother, Mike, with fiancée, Audra, were there—a first, apparently—invited by Natalie, whose skill as a detective Vera was growing to admire greatly. Natalie, it turned out, was getting married to her college sweetheart, Matt Shaffer, on June fourteenth, just two short weeks away. Matt was there standing next to her, looking all tall and lean and muscular like the security chief he was.

Hanging a bit back, observing the crowd, was another man, Austin Dearing, whom Vera immediately recognized from the tabloids. Brawny, tan, chiseled as a sculpture and built like a Delta Force god, he and Vera's friend Silver had created quite the scandal last month by announcing first their baby, and *then* their whirlwind marriage.

Silver was the first to come over and give Vera a big welcome hug. "You and Conner!" Silver exclaimed with a grin. "What a surprise!"

She had no idea.

They were immediately joined by the only cousin Vera hadn't already met. Jenna, the youngest of the half sisters, who was Vera's age. Jenna was an event planner, party princess, an absolute knockout and clearly the apple of her daddy's eye. Harold's gaze followed her proudly from the foot of the foyer staircase as she said hello to Vera then was drawn into the midst of the other arriving guests.

For a family dinner, there was quite a crowd gathering. Through which Conner expertly steered her, until they got to the staircase and Harold Rothchild, who'd been joined with perfect timing by his current wife, Rebecca.

Harold gave Conner a slap on the back. "Glad you could make it, boy. Come see who's here."

Vera saw Conner pale when he turned and found himself eye-to-eye with Michael and Emily Rothchild, his parents. Uh-oh. He *hadn't* been expecting that.

"Thought it was time to bury the hatchet," Harold said, then sobered. "When Candace died, I realized what was important in life. And that's family." He turned to Conner and lightened up. "Isn't that right, boy?" He slapped him on the back again.

Conner glanced over at her. She smiled, so filled with love for the man she was bursting at the seams. Even as he fought for his own happiness, he never forgot his love and duty to his parents and family. Never forgot that his decisions affected more than himself, or even her. It made her love him all the more to know he was willing to sacrifice for his family. She'd never known that kind of loyalty and was awed that it was now all directed toward her.

As was his attention. He held out his hand to her, she took it and he pulled her up the staircase a few steps, so he towered over the noisy throng crowding the massive foyer.

He let out a piercing whistle. The talking and laughing stopped abruptly. Everyone turned to stare at him in surprised expectation. Suddenly, her knees felt weak. *Oh, God.* This was worse than dangling a hundred feet over a cliff.

Okay, not really. But almost.

But his gaze met hers, and she could feel all the love and support she'd need for a whole lifetime pouring through them into her. He squeezed her hand. Then turned to the crowd.

"Before we go in to dinner, I'd like to introduce someone very special to me." He glanced at his parents and uncle. "Mom, Dad, this is Vera. Uncle Harold, you invited us here tonight because you wanted to meet my young lady. Well, I'm afraid that's not possible." Harold's bushy brows rose. "You see," Conner continued, "Vera is no longer my young lady. As of an hour ago, she's much more to me than that."

Gasps went through the room. He smiled down at her.

"Everyone, I'd like you to meet Vera Mancuso Rothchild. My new wife."

Epilogue

Two weeks later

Tears trickled down Vera's cheeks as she watched Natalie Rothchild and Matt Shaffer say their wedding vows. The church was packed, and there wasn't a dry eye in the house. Natalie and Matt had written the words themselves, and there was no doubt in Vera's mind that they meant every single word. It was movingly beautiful, the whole ceremony.

Afterward, as the organ music swelled and everyone stood wiping tears and cheering the bride and groom out of the church, Vera realized Conner, who'd held her left hand in both of his the whole time, was watching her instead.

She gave him a watery smile, dabbing with a tissue. "I'm such a sucker for weddings," she said with a happy sigh.

He raised her hand to his lips, kissing her ring finger, where two weeks ago he'd placed a simple gold band. "Are you sorry?" he asked softly, his eyes filled with emotion. "That I didn't give you a day like this? With flowers and a white dress and a big party? A day to remember for the rest of your life…"

She met his gaze, and her eyes brimmed over anew. Didn't he know stopping at that Vegas wedding chapel on the way to dinner at the Rothchilds had been the happiest moment of her entire life? The shock, the utter joy, the amazing realization that he truly loved her, wanted to spend his life with her, was worth more than anything in the universe.

"Oh, Conner. You *did* give me a day to remember for the rest of my life. I wouldn't have changed a thing. Not one. Not for the world."

He bent down and kissed her tenderly. "Sure?"

She gently touched his cheek. "Positive." She smiled. "And believe me, the white dress thing? Been there, done that. Not a big deal."

His lips curved up at that, as she'd hoped they would. She kissed him lovingly. "Conner, don't think for a single moment that—"

"Hey, you two," an amused male voice interrupted from behind Conner. "No smooching in church. You're holding up traffic."

She rolled her eyes at Lex Duncan, who'd sat next to them in the pew. It was their turn to exit. "You're just jealous because you didn't bring a date to smooch with."

He made a face. "Date? Remind me again what that is?" He followed them out of the church into the bright sunshine. "Aside from which, technically, I'm working."

Conner shook his head. "Buddy, you need to forget that job of yours for an afternoon and take advantage." He swept an appreciative glance around. "Check out all the gorgeous women, all dressed up and all choked up on love, just waiting for a handsome man such as yourself to make their dreams come true. Have you never seen *The Wedding Crashers?*"

Duncan gave a short laugh. "Funny. Anyway, I don't dare get distracted. Aside from keeping watch for our escaped stalker, I'm deathly afraid war is going to break out at any moment."

Conner winced. "You mean among the guests?"

Duncan nodded, surveying the large area in front of the church where the reception line was forming.

Vera looked, too. "What do you mean?"

Conner put his arm around her and squeezed. "Your new brother-in-law comes from the biggest mob family in Las Vegas. See all the hard-eyed men in dark suits? And you can't miss the sea of khaki uniforms."

True. Half the Metro force had turned out for the wedding of one of their own. And Matt had mentioned his notorious family on a couple of occasions.

"Yikes," she said. "I hadn't thought of that."

"I better get to work."

As Duncan left, Natalie's sister Jenna came up and gave Conner a kiss on the cheek. "Don't worry, cuz. Matt assures me his family will be on their best behavior."

Jenna had done an amazing job putting together the whole wedding. Her eyes scanned the proceedings critically, never resting, ready to head off any problem before it arose.

"The church flowers were lovely, Jenna," Vera said. "Everything was so gorgeous."

"Thanks. Wait'll you see the reception hall. Dad gave me an unlimited budget." She grinned. "I took blatant advantage. But speaking of receptions, you two are wanted in the reception line now. Get your butts over there."

"Us?" Vera asked in alarm.

"Favorite cousin, and all." Jenna's eyes landed on Duncan's

receding back. "Say, who was that guy? I thought I knew everyone on the guest list."

"Lex Duncan. The FBI agent who's been helping us with the Tears of the Quetzal. He just took over Candace's case, too."

Vera secretly winked at Conner. "Handsome, isn't he? And single, too."

Jenna's gaze lingered appreciatively on him for a second, then moved on distractedly. "Whatever. Come on, you two. Reception line."

Terrified at the prospect, Vera looked to Conner for support. "I really don't think—"

"Nonsense. It's time I introduced my wife to society. No time like the present."

Jenna smiled encouragingly. "It'll be fine."

And as it turned out, it was. More than fine.

When they joined the line right next to Conner's parents, his father shook Vera's hand and kissed her cheek, and his mother actually hugged her. The first couple of days after Conner's surprise announcement at dinner had been rocky. But they'd been more shell-shocked than disapproving. Once they accepted the idea of a married son, they'd made an honest effort to get to know his new wife. That was all Vera could ask, and it seemed like they had accepted her, too.

His parents weren't the only ones stunned by the news that Conner Rothchild had gotten married. He did, after all, have a reputation as a confirmed bachelor who played the field with gusto. She'd learned that was mostly media hype, a facade cultivated to help his tireless work for those less fortunate than himself. Nothing like society connections to change society. But even his close friends were surprised. When had a workaholic like him had time to fall in love?

Sixty seconds was all it took, he'd assured them all. One look, and he was a goner.

There were a few sideways glances at Vera from those guests who'd heard about her questionable background. But there were many more who'd read about the press conference Maximillian St. Giles had held about Darla and Henry, and his unexpected announcement that he'd discovered he had another daughter, one who had risked her life to save his other children. And that he'd acknowledged being her father and written her into his will as an equal heir to the other two.

Congratulations flowed from both sides, Conner couldn't stop beaming and her heart was filled with joy.

Talk about a Cinderella moment.

Things like this *did* happen to people like her!

"I am so incredibly happy," she said to Conner when they were in the Batmobile, driving to the reception, which was being held at the Rothchild Grand Hotel. "How did I get so lucky to find you?"

He grinned over at her. "Uncle Harold said it must be the curse of the Tears of the Quetzal. Or in this case, the blessing. Rothchilds are falling like dominoes. In love, that is."

She grinned back. "Well, it's true, I *was* wearing the ring the first time I saw you," she teased as they pulled in at the Grand.

"That's about *all* you were wearing," he teased back. "Who could help falling in love with you at first sight? Every last man in the room was in love with you." He pulled into the parking lot, leaned over to grasp her behind the neck and kissed her. "I was just the lucky guy who got you all for myself."

"Yes," she said, loving the taste of her new husband, loving the feel of his muscular body, loving the honor in his heart most of all. "You did."

The wedding party limo pulled up with a blare of horns and a rippling of crepe paper bunting. Natalie and Matt emerged, glowing and smiling and kissing like two people so in love the earth spun around the axis of it. Just like Vera and Conner.

She returned his kiss with all the love within her heart and soul. Then told him sincerely, "Flowers and white dresses and parties are wonderful, darling. But none of those things matter. We already have what's important. We have each other, and we have love. I love you so much, Conner. That's all I'll ever need."

His eyes looked down at her so tenderly her heart simply overflowed. "I love you, too, Vera. So very much."

Again, he raised her fingers to his lips and kissed them, and then he slipped another ring on next to her wedding band.

She looked down at it in surprise. A perfect diamond winked back at her, blazing with green, purple and blue sparkles. Just like a miniature Quetzal.

"So we can make our own magic," he whispered. And kissed her again.

Oh, yes. The magic of love.

* * * * *

Celebrate 60 years of pure reading pleasure with Harlequin!

To commemorate the event, Harlequin Intrigue® is thrilled to invite you to the wedding of The Colby Agency's J. T. Baxley and his bride, Eve Mattson.

That is, of course, if J.T. can find the woman who left him at the altar. Considering he's a private investigator for one of the top agencies in the country—the best of the best—that shouldn't be a problem. The real setback is that his bride isn't who she appears to be…and her mysterious past has put them both in danger.

Enjoy an exclusive glimpse of Debra Webb's latest addition to
THE COLBY AGENCY: ELITE
RECONNAISSANCE DIVISION

THE BRIDE'S SECRETS

Available August 2009 from Harlequin Intrigue®.

The dark figures on the dock were still firing. The bullets cutting through the surface of the water without the warning boom of shots told Eve they were using silencers.

That was to her benefit. Silencers decreased the accuracy of every shot and lessened the range.

She grabbed for the rocks. Scrambled through the darkness. Bumped her knee on a boulder. Cursed.

Burrowing into the waist-deep grass, she kept low and crawled forward. Faster. Pushed harder. Needed as much distance as possible.

Shots pinged on the rocks.

J.T. scrambled alongside her.

He was breathing hard.

They had to stay close to the ground until they reached the next row of warehouses. Even though she was relatively certain they were out of range at this point, she wasn't taking any risks. And she wasn't slowing down.

J.T. had to keep up.

The splat of a bullet hitting the ground next to Eve had her rolling left. Maybe they weren't completely out of range.

She bumped J.T. He grunted.

His injured arm. Dammit. She could apologize later.

Half a dozen more yards.

Almost in the clear.

As she reached the cover of the alley between the first two warehouses she tensed.

Silence.

No pings or splats.

She glanced back at the dock. Deserted.

Time to run.

Her car was parked another block down.

Pushing to her feet, she sprinted forward. The wet bag dragged at her shoulder. She ignored it.

By the time she reached the lot where her car was parked, she had dug the keys from her pocket and hit the fob. Six seconds later she was behind the wheel. She hit the ignition as J.T. collapsed into the passenger seat. Tires squealed as she spun out of the slot.

"What the hell did you do to me?"

From the corner of her eye she watched him shake his head in an attempt to clear it.

He would be pissed when she told him about the tranquilizer.

She'd needed him cooperative until she formulated a plan. A drug-induced state of unconsciousness had been the fastest and most efficient method to ensure his continued solidarity.

"I can't really talk right now." Eve weaved into the right lane as the street widened to four lanes. What she needed was traffic. It was Saturday night—shouldn't be that difficult to find as soon as they were out of the old warehouse district.

A glance in the rearview mirror warned that their unwanted company had caught up.

Sensing her tension, J.T. turned to peer over his left shoulder.

"I hope you have a plan B."

She shot him a look. "There's always plan G." Then she pulled the Glock out of her waistband.

Cutting the steering wheel left, she slid between two vehicles. Another veer to the right and she'd put several cars between hers and the enemy.

She was betting they wouldn't pull out the firepower in the open like this, but a girl could never be too sure when it came to an unknown enemy.

Deep blending was the way to go.

Two traffic lights ahead the marquis of a movie theater provided exactly the opportunity she was looking for.

The digital numbers on the dash indicated it was just past midnight. Perfect timing. The late movie would be purging its audience into the crowd of teenagers who liked hanging out in the parking lot.

She took a hard right onto the property that sported a twelve-screen theater, numerous fast-food hot spots and a chain superstore. Speeding across the lot, she selected a lane of parking slots. Pulling in as close to the theater entrance as possible, she shut off the engine and reached for her door.

"Let's go."

Thankfully he didn't argue.

Rounding the hood of her car, she shoved the Glock into her bag, then wrapped her arm around J.T.'s and merged into the crowd.

With her free hand she finger-combed her long hair. It was soaked, as were her clothes. The kids she bumped into noticed, gave her death-ray glares.

They just didn't know.

As she and J.T. moved in closer to the building, she grabbed a baseball cap from an innocent bystander. The crowd made it easy. The kid who owned the cap had made it even easier by stuffing the cap bill-first into his waistband at the small of his back.

Pushing through the loitering crowd, she made her way to the side of the building next to the main entrance. She pushed J.T. against the wall and dropped her bag to the ground. Peeled off her tee and let it fall.

His gaze instantly zeroed in on her breasts, where the cami she wore had glued to her skin like an extra layer. A zing of desire shot through her veins.

Not the time.

With a flick of her wrist she twisted her hair up and clamped the cap atop the blond mass.

"They're coming," J.T. muttered as he gazed at some point beyond her.

"Yeah, I know." She planted her palms against the wall on either side of him and leaned in. "Keep your eyes open. Let me know when they're inside."

Then she planted her lips on his.

* * * * *

Will J.T. and Eve be caught in the moment?
Or will Eve get the chance to reveal all of her secrets?
Find out in
THE BRIDE'S SECRETS
by Debra Webb
Available August 2009 from Harlequin Intrigue®

We'll be spotlighting a different series every month throughout 2009 to celebrate our 60th anniversary.

LOOK FOR HARLEQUIN INTRIGUE® IN AUGUST!

To commemorate the event, Harlequin Intrigue® is thrilled to invite you to the wedding of the Colby Agency's J. T. Baxley and his bride, Eve Mattson.

Look for *Colby Agency: Elite Reconnaissance*

THE BRIDE'S SECRETS
BY DEBRA WEBB

Available August 2009

www.eHarlequin.com

You're invited to join our Tell Harlequin Reader Panel!

By joining our new reader panel you will:

- Receive Harlequin® books—they are FREE and yours to keep with no obligation to purchase anything!
- Participate in fun online surveys
- Exchange opinions and ideas with women just like you
- Have a say in our new book ideas and help us publish the best in women's fiction

In addition, you will have a chance to win great prizes and receive special gifts!
See Web site for details. Some conditions apply.
Space is limited.

To join, visit us at
www.TellHarlequin.com.

REQUEST YOUR FREE BOOKS!

2 FREE NOVELS PLUS 2 FREE GIFTS!

Silhouette® Romantic SUSPENSE

Sparked by Danger, Fueled by Passion!

YES! Please send me 2 FREE Silhouette® Romantic Suspense novels and my 2 FREE gifts (gifts are worth about $10). After receiving them, if I don't wish to receive any more books, I can return the shipping statement marked "cancel." If I don't cancel, I will receive 4 brand-new novels every month and be billed just $4.24 per book in the U.S. or $4.99 per book in Canada. That's a savings of at least 15% off the cover price! It's quite a bargain! Shipping and handling is just 50¢ per book*. I understand that accepting the 2 free books and gifts places me under no obligation to buy anything. I can always return a shipment and cancel at any time. Even if I never buy another book from Silhouette, the two free books and gifts are mine to keep forever.

240 SDN EYL4 340 SDN EYMG

Name	(PLEASE PRINT)

Address	Apt. #

City	State/Prov.	Zip/Postal Code

Signature (if under 18, a parent or guardian must sign)

Mail to the **Silhouette Reader Service:**
IN U.S.A.: P.O. Box 1867, Buffalo, NY 14240-1867
IN CANADA: P.O. Box 609, Fort Erie, Ontario L2A 5X3

Not valid to current subscribers of Silhouette Romantic Suspense books.

Want to try two free books from another line?
Call 1-800-873-8635 or visit www.morefreebooks.com.

* Terms and prices subject to change without notice. Prices do not include applicable taxes. Sales tax applicable in N.Y. Canadian residents will be charged applicable provincial taxes and GST. Offer not valid in Quebec. This offer is limited to one order per household. All orders subject to approval. Credit or debit balances in a customer's account(s) may be offset by any other outstanding balance owed by or to the customer. Please allow 4 to 6 weeks for delivery. Offer available while quantities last.

Your Privacy: Silhouette is committed to protecting your privacy. Our Privacy Policy is available online at www.eHarlequin.com or upon request from the Reader Service. From time to time we make our lists of customers available to reputable third parties who may have a product or service of interest to you. If you would prefer we not share your name and address, please check here. ☐

SRS09R

Stay up-to-date on all your romance reading news!

The Harlequin Inside Romance newsletter is a **FREE** quarterly newsletter highlighting our upcoming series releases and promotions!

Go to
eHarlequin.com/InsideRomance
or e-mail us at
InsideRomance@Harlequin.com
to sign up to receive
your FREE newsletter today!

In 2009 Harlequin celebrates
60 years of pure reading pleasure!

We're marking this occasion by offering
16 **FREE** full books to download and read.

Visit

www.HarlequinCelebrates.com

to choose from a variety of
great romance stories
that are absolutely **FREE!**

(Total approximate retail value of $60)

We invite you to visit and share the Web site
with your friends, family
and anyone who enjoys reading.

Silhouette®
Romantic
SUSPENSE

COMING NEXT MONTH

Available July 28, 2009

#1571 CAVANAUGH PRIDE—Marie Ferrarella
Cavanaugh Justice
When detective Julianne White Bear is sent from another town to
help hunt a serial killer, she brings with her a secret motive. Detective
Frank McIntyre has his hands full heading the task force, but he can't
deny his attraction toward Julianne—and the feeling is mutual. They're
determined to put romance on hold until justice is served, but it isn't
always that easy….

#1572 HER 24-HOUR PROTECTOR—Loreth Anne White
Love in 60 Seconds
FBI agent Lex Duncan and casino heiress Jenna Rothchild play each other
from the moment they meet. Even as the heat between the two sizzles
hotter than the Las Vegas desert, danger intensifies around them. Suddenly
Lex becomes the one man who can rescue the sexy young heiress…in
more ways than one.

#1573 HIS PERSONAL MISSION—Justine Davis
Redstone, Incorporated
Ryan Barton's teenage sister is missing, and his only hope to find her is
Sasha Tereschenko—the woman he'd loved and lost two years ago. Family
is everything to Sasha, who leaps into action. While the two track down the
predator possibly holding Ryan's sister, their former attraction arises again,
and their lives—and hearts—are put at risk.

#1574 SILENT WATCH—Elle Kennedy
Samantha Dawson has been in hiding since the night of her brutal attack.
Now, living in isolation under a new identity, she is surprised to find a sexy
FBI agent on her doorstep. Blake Corwin promises to protect Samantha in
exchange for her help with her attacker's latest victim. But the last thing he
expected was to fall for Sam, and when she again becomes a target, Blake
will do anything to save her.

SRSCNMBPA0709